CAPTIVATED

TEN TALES OF WILLING AND THRILLING SUBMISSION

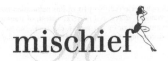

mischief

Mischief
An imprint of HarperCollins*Publishers*
77–85 Fulham Palace Road,
Hammersmith, London W6 8JB

www.mischiefbooks.com

A Paperback Original 2013

First published in Great Britain in ebook format by
HarperCollins*Publishers* 2012

Copyright
For My Own Good © Justine Elyot
Best in Show © Lolita Lopez
Seventeen Brass Circles © Sommer Marsden
I Am © Charlotte Stein
My Night as a Sex Slave © Valerie Grey
Minding Rex © Elizabeth Coldwell
The Breaking of Sub Paul © Kyoko Church
Runaway © Heather Towne
Confessions of a Coffee Slave © Lisette Ashton
Dominant Skin © Aishling Morgan

The author asserts the moral right to
be identified as the author of this work

A catalogue record for this book is
available from the British Library

ISBN-13: 9780007553198

Find out more about HarperCollins and the environment at
www.harpercollins.co.uk/green

CONTENTS

Contents

For My Own Good
Justine Elyot

'This is really what you want?'

I suppose the question had to be asked, but the posing of it made me doubt myself for a moment. Was it? Really?

I looked at the cage in the corner of the room. It was such an elegant thing, the bars highly polished and shining, the interior decorated in a style best described as 'harem luxe'. I had seen this cage in my dreams.

His hands were on my shoulders and I nuzzled his knuckles with my cheeks.

'You know it's for my own good,' I told him. 'I'm not safe on the streets.'

A soft laugh came from above.

'That's true enough. Well, then. If you're sure.'

He took my arm and led me over to the open gate.

Before I could crawl in, there were some formalities to be observed. First, the blindfold, then the handcuffs.

I entered the cage on my knees, shuffling forward into a world of velvets and silks that was all dark to me, my fingers twisting behind my back. I reached what felt like a central area and sat down, my knees drawn up to my chin, waiting.

I heard the cage door slam, a key turned, some bolts slid across.

Then I heard footsteps, retreating, the soft click of the door beyond.

I was alone. Have I mentioned that I was naked?

Now was my chance to soak into my role. I had been taken. Not kidnapped, not arrested, not even abducted but taken, spirited out of my life in a bid to save me from some worse fate. The point of this captivity, the thing that excited me the most about it, was that it was being done in the name of love and protection.

After a while, who knows how long, I lay down on my side. The room temperature was warm but my nipples felt engorged anyway, perhaps with anticipation. I tried to become the girl taken from the streets by an unseen captor, the helpless, heedless creature meant for enslavement, if only she knew it.

By the time the door opened again, I was there, in the space I'd craved, ready to inhabit it fully.

'Who are you? Where is this?' My voice sounded lost and foolish in the dark. I sat up and hugged my arms around me, facing the direction of the footsteps.

'I thought you might be hungry. Come over to me.'

I recognised the speaker. It was someone I was supposed to fear.

'Oh, it's you! What have you done with me? You'd better let me go or …'

'Sh. Come over to me.'

'I don't want to.'

'Come over here or I'll make you. It wouldn't be difficult. And I have food.'

My stomach was empty, it was true. After a moment's hesitation, I capitulated and moved in the direction of his voice.

'Why are you doing this?' My nipples reached the bars first, brushing the cold steel, which did nothing to reduce their size.

'You'll understand, in time.'

'I want to understand now.'

'Patience,' he said.

I heard a spoon scrape against china, then the tip of the metal touched my lower lip. I smelled porridge, milky with perhaps a sprinkling of sugar. I opened my mouth, irritated by my own obedience, but wanting to taste and swallow and banish the nagging emptiness from my stomach.

He pushed the spoon inside my mouth and waited for me to lick off the last remnants of porridge before removing it.

3

'That's it,' he said softly. 'It's good for you. Eat it up.'

He continued to feed me until I felt enough strength to resist him and I stopped opening my mouth.

'No, finish it,' he reproved, trying to force the curved metal between my teeth.

I shook my head, turned my face away.

'Oh, Phoebe, you will make me come in there. You don't want that.'

Actually, I *did* want that, and I supposed he knew it, but I was enjoying the pleasurable tension too much to break it just yet.

'What's it to you if I leave some porridge?'

'It's a great deal to me. For one thing, I need you in good health. For another, you must learn to be obedient or this is going to be very hard for you.'

'What is? What is *this*?'

'You only need to know that you are here for your own safety and protection. More than that, I probably shouldn't say.'

'You certainly should. It's my life! I deserve an explanation.'

'Eat your porridge and perhaps I'll give you one.'

I sighed and let him feed me once more.

'Well?' I said, once the final morsel was dispatched.

'I only said perhaps.'

'Fuck you!'

He heaved a sigh.

'I'm going to have to come in there, aren't I?'

I shuffled back rapidly, but he reached through the bars and held my face by the chin, halting me.

'Wait there,' he said. 'Don't try anything.'

There wasn't much I could try, cuffed and unseeing, but I tried to follow the direction of his footsteps and drag myself over to where I thought the gate must be, once he started clanking it.

'I said wait there,' he warned. 'Tut tut, somebody is really asking for trouble, isn't she?'

The gate was open. I tried to hurl myself at it, but found myself hard up against his body, caught in his grip immediately. He held my arm tightly while he locked us both in. I tried to work out what he did with the key, but I couldn't.

'Now then, Phoebe,' he said. He held both of my arms. The material of his clothes brushed against my nipples, reinforcing the power dynamic. He got to wear things. I didn't. 'What is this nonsense?'

'That's my question!' I cried. 'You can't keep me prisoner.'

'It's not my fault,' he said. 'You were in danger. I knew you wouldn't come with me if I asked you to. I had to take you.'

'What sort of danger?'

'Never mind what sort of danger.'

'But I do mind! Of course I mind.'

5

He silenced me with a kiss, which I tried at first to resist, to all the more appreciate the sweetness of surrender when it came, as it inevitably did. His kisses were nourishment to me, much more than any food or drink. I would take them where I found them.

Once I was quiet and docile, he held me to him and said, 'You understand that you're where you need to be?'

'I don't understand anything.'

'But you'll behave yourself? Or do I need to show you what happens when you don't?'

My pussy clenched, clit bursting into full bloom.

I had always liked his consequences for bad behaviour.

'Why don't you take off these handcuffs?' I asked. 'And the blindfold?'

'I can't trust you yet. You'll try something.'

'What the hell can I try stuck inside a cage?'

'I don't know. You'll think of something. Perhaps we really do need that lesson in what happens if you do.'

'I won't do anything,' I said quickly.

'No, because you'll have this to think about if you're tempted,' he said.

Before I could argue, I was bent over his thighs, held down by his hand in the small of my back.

'Oh, don't,' I whimpered, but that was nowhere near our safe word, so he took no notice and the first hard smack of many landed on my upturned bottom.

Through the pain I wanted him to say the words, the words that always drove me wild, the words I craved and dreamt of in my fantasies.

But he said other things instead, things about obedience and submission, about duty and discipline.

My bottom got hotter and I thought about trying to wriggle off him, but first he had to say the words.

'You mustn't resist me, Phoebe. You know this is for your own good.'

Oh, he had said them and I could stop struggling and lift my bum higher, asking for more.

He was happy to give it, and eventually I was scorched all over and my skin was tight and stinging. He stopped then, and rested his palm on the curve of my cheeks.

'I take it you understand?' he said.

'Yes,' I whispered, needing to be touched. I shimmied my hips encouragingly.

'Good. I'll be back when you're in a more accommodating frame of mind.'

'What? You're going?'

'Just for a little while. Perhaps you'll miss me.'

I was damn sure I would.

I tried to keep him close, but all he needed to do was gently push me off him and down on to the cushions.

'Can't you take off these cuffs now?' I pleaded.

'Not yet. Later.' He patted my sore bottom. 'I'm going to give you some time to think about this first.'

7

I couldn't even touch it. More to the point, I couldn't even touch anything else, specifically my clit.

I heard the gate shut and the key turn and then he left.

I lay on my side in a torment of frustrated desire. I clamped my thighs tight together and tried to generate enough friction to set things in motion, but it was useless. The heat of my behind worked wonderfully well at swelling my clit and making my juices run, but it couldn't take anything further than that.

I lay on my stomach, trying to grind into the deep-pile fabrics, spreading my legs wide and rubbing myself on them. This seemed to work quite well, especially when I found a position and rhythm I could be comfortable with. I swivelled my hips over the cushions, wondering if I would get into trouble for this. Would he find out? Would he discover a telltale patch of damp on one of the sumptuous silks that would doom me to punishment?

And what if he did?

I wouldn't be unhappy about it.

I scissored my thighs together, clamping a big fat pillow between them, humping it with determination. I was thus engaged when the door opened again.

I had to stop, though I was so close, so tormentingly close. I hid my face in the fabrics and muffled a moan.

'Goodness me.' His footsteps approached. 'Whatever do we have here?'

I held myself perfectly still, unable to answer.

'It looks as if somebody needs something quite badly. Is that right?'

I made an incoherent sound, biting on a tassel.

'Answer me, Phoebe.'

'Yes.'

'Get up on your knees and answer properly. I'm not underneath that cushion, am I?'

Unwillingly, I made the effort to raise myself, not so easy without the use of my hands. My shame-stained face directed at him, I whispered, 'Yes,' again.

'And what is it that you need? Tell me.'

'I need to come.'

'Why do you need to come, Phoebe?'

'Because ... I'm a bit ... aroused.'

'A *bit* aroused?'

'Quite a lot aroused.'

'I can tell. How did that happen, then? What aroused you?'

His footsteps travelled the perimeter of the cage. I followed them with my ears, moving my neck in sympathy.

'I think ... I don't know.'

I lost my nerve at the last minute. I knew he wouldn't stand for that.

'You don't know? How can you not know what turns you on?'

'I do know. I don't want to say.'

'Well, you don't have the choice. You have to tell me. Especially if you ever want those cuffs off. So?'

'It was because of what you did to me.'

'Oh.' I could hear the weight of pleasure and triumph in his voice, even though I knew this wouldn't be specific enough. 'What I did to you. I see. And what was that?'

'You …' I stopped to heave a heavy sigh. He knew this was always the most difficult part of a scene for me. The naming of things. The speaking out loud of my innermost secrets.

'I can see I'll have to come in there,' he said.

'You hurt me.'

'You like pain? So, if I twist your arm, that'll turn you on?'

'No.' If my hands had been free, I would have wrung them.

'What then?'

'It was the way you did it.'

'With my hands?'

'Yes.' His hands. Always so accurate in the distribution of pain and pleasure, or both together.

'My hands where?'

My fingers interlocked and I held them there, gripping tight.

'On my bottom.'

'Aha. Yes. And what's that called, then, Phoebe? What's it called when my hand makes sharp contact with your bottom?'

10

I could say it now. Each exchange of words had laid the pathway and now I had the nerve to speak.

'A spanking.'

'Good girl.' I could almost see his smile, his eyes crinkling at the corners, his white teeth. 'And that's what turned you on, is it?'

'Yes.'

'Well, it's not much of a punishment then, is it? Perhaps I'll have to think of something else. But, now we've established what it was that made you want to treat the cushions so ... inappropriately, we have another issue to address, don't we?'

'Do we?'

'Oh yes. You see, I'm very pleased with you, Phoebe. I'm very pleased that I've got you here in this little cage, with me, where you belong. You seem to understand that now. You seem to have come round. Am I right?'

'I ... don't know.' I didn't want to admit defeat yet.

'Wait. I'm coming in there.'

The keys, the door, the slam, the lock.

Where was he? I tried to locate him by sound, then by smell, but I didn't know where he was until he untied the blindfold, releasing me into blurred brightness.

The cuffs came off next, but he held on to my wrists, massaging them. They were a little numb and I had pins and needles in my hands.

'I think you're going to behave yourself,' he said,

11

rubbing away. 'I hope you will justify my trust, because, if you don't, I'll be very disappointed. And I don't take disappointment well.'

'Why am I here?' I asked again.

'Because I want you to be here.'

I twisted my neck round, able to look at him now. He stopped the massage and put his hands on my shoulders, pushing his thumbs into the back of my neck.

'So,' he said, soft and low, 'when you get spanked, you like it. How does it make you feel?'

'Warm. Powerless. Safe. Tingly.'

'So it's partly what I do to you, and partly how you respond to that?'

'I suppose. I feel like I'm programmed to respond in a certain way.'

'You don't get scared?'

'Not really. Unless I think you're never going to stop.'

'Perhaps that'll happen one day. Perhaps I just won't stop.'

He knew I liked a thrill of fear with my sex sometimes. I appreciated his attempt to bring it back.

I bathed in the frisson, throwing back my head, nuzzling his neck.

'The question is,' he said, 'what am I going to do with you? You get horny when I spank you and try to hump the décor. We can't have that, can we?'

'I don't know.'

'No, we can't. I suppose I'll have to service you, won't I? Not that I mind. It was all part of the plan, after all. I'm just surprised you've been so quick and easy. Is that what you are, Phoebe? Easy?'

I am for you.

'No, of course not.'

'But you want it, don't you? You want me to show you what you're here for.'

There was no point denying it. I nodded.

'Oh, Phoebe, you're the best prisoner ever,' he said, and without ceremony he bent me over so my spine was curved and my face fell into the pillows.

He pushed apart my thighs and I felt his breath on my cunt, his face down low, examining me.

'Still a little bit red,' he said, stroking my bum. 'I like that. But you're very wet, you know. Incredibly wet. Is this what being caged does for you?'

'I suppose it might be.'

'No suppose about it.' He scooped some juices out with a finger. 'This is one very turned-on little slut, just here.'

He reached between my spread lips, fingering my clit.

'This is going to work out so well,' he said, stroking away, while I quivered my hips beneath his touch. 'You get to stay safe and be looked after and taken care of and given a good seeing-to whenever you need it. I get what I've always wanted. A pussy that's wet for me, all the time. That's how it'll be, don't you think?'

'Yes, yes.'

'It's going to be so good.'

It was already so good. I was vibrating under him, pushing myself into his fingertips. I began to pant, preparing for take-off, but he smacked my thigh and tutted.

'So impatient. Wait for me.'

He unbuckled his belt, sorted out his trousers. I eased backwards into the welcome nudge of his cock. He moved his hands to my breasts, playing with my nipples while he slid all the way in.

'Did you know I was hard?' he murmured in my ear.

'No.'

'You do now. Why do you think I was? What made me hard?'

'Seeing me here. In your cage, naked.'

'I can't deny it, it's quite a sight. It's not all, though. The thing is, Phoebe, I'm always hard around you. Clothed or naked, caged or free. I only have to lay eyes on you to want to … lay you.'

'Is that why you took me?'

'It's to do with that, yes. I have to have you here, ready and waiting for me. Just the thought of you, all trussed up and behind bars, with a pussy that needs filling … oh, God. I have to keep still a moment.'

He had been circling his hips, grinding round and round inside me. He stopped, gasping slightly, controlling himself, and me.

'I've thought about this for years,' he said levelly.

Then he began to thrust, deep strokes that made me know I was here to satisfy and serve him.

'But I never wanted to suggest it,' he continued, pounding on.

I held on to the silk, crumpling it in my fists.

'Until, one day, you brought it up yourself. I couldn't believe my luck.'

The steady screwing was having its effect. I made little whimpering noises. He pinched my nipples then left them alone, moving his hands lower down. One held me at my hip while the other wriggled between my arse cheeks. He brushed it down, moving past the ever-thrusting obstacle of his cock in my cunt and dipping it into my wetness. I wanted him to stay near my clit, but, once his fingers were slippery, he moved them back to my bottom.

I knew then what was coming.

The sharp stab of a fingertip invading my sphincter made me flinch, but only momentarily, because it was welcome. He fucked on steadily while his finger made its examination of my tight rear passage. He understood what this did to me, where it took me.

I became more vocal, rotating my pelvis in a delirium of lust.

As he pushed a second finger up, he put his mouth to my ear. 'You know this is for your own good, don't you?' he said.

I had to take it and I had to give in to an epic climax that burst behind my eyes like stars. When I gave him my orgasm, I gave him all of myself. I was his slave, and not because he had caged me, but because he could make me feel like this, whenever he wanted to.

He gripped my shoulder with his other hand and poured himself into me, hissing victoriously until he was drained.

The cushions would be ruined, but it didn't seem to matter.

We lay together, banked in velvet and silk, looking up at the barred roof.

'What if this was real?' he said.

'I thought it was.'

'What if I kept you in here and never let you out?'

'Would you want to do that?'

'Would it even be possible?'

'I think I'd quite like it. As long as you let me out to shower and stuff like that. There's the TV over there, I could have some music, some books. It's pretty comfortable.'

'You'd be waiting here, while I was at work, thinking of me.'

'I'd always be thinking of you. The cage would do that for me.'

'Waiting for me to get home. Mmm.'

He shut his eyes, reaching out for me, rolling me against him.

'I like the idea of it,' I said. 'I like the idea of being your on-call pleasure slave.'

'So do I. Well, let's see if we can make some time to do something like that then. Let's synchronise diaries.'

I laughed. 'Block in some face time.'

'Slave time.'

'Yes, that would be good. It would be for my own good.'

Best in Show
Lolita Lopez

'Who's a good girl?' Mark teased in a singsong voice as he ruffled my hair and plopped a pair of puppy ears on the crown of my head.

I dared to glare over at him as he adjusted the headband so the ears sat evenly. I wasn't exactly thrilled by the night's activities he had planned for us, but it was his birthday so I was feeling a bit generous. 'I can't believe I'm doing this.'

Mark smiled down at me and lovingly stroked my cheek. 'You're doing this because you love me and because I'm your master. You want to please your master, don't you?'

My belly wobbled as he spoke to me in that firm, low voice of his that I loved so much. My need to submit, to find pleasure in serving him, trumped my embarrassment at wearing this ridiculous puppy outfit. I wasn't quite sure where my desperate need to serve and submit originated. I just knew that the first moment Mark had spoken to me at a friend's cocktail party, I'd been immediately enthralled. He'd slowly and carefully introduced me to the world of dominance and submission and exposed me to a lifestyle I'd always secretly craved. It was no coincidence that my bedroom bookshelves were packed with BDSM-themed erotica. It had simply taken Mark to help me take that interest from the realm of imagination to reality.

We maintained a delicate balance in our relationship. Although we enjoyed our fair share of domestic discipline and were flirting with total power exchange, we lived the unremarkable life of any modern couple. Outside the house and these types of play parties, we existed as two fully independent and successful people. Mark wasn't the least bit intimidated by my earning power either. As a lead research and development scientist at a growing biotech company, I easily trumped his take-home pay as a detective. In a way, the roles we assumed in the bedroom were the complete opposite of the ones we played out in society. I rather liked it that way.

'Here,' Mark said and picked up the mittens from the centre console of his SUV. 'Give me your hands.'

I reluctantly stuck them out and allowed him to slide the silly-looking leather mittens over my hands. As he fastened them at my wrists, I studied my new paws. They looked similar to the leather bootees on my feet and were both functional and decorative. Apparently they were supposed to protect and cushion my hands while I crawled around on all floors and pretended to be a good puppy. Mark had even gone so far as to buy me a pair of kneepads from the fetish-wear shop where he'd picked up the rest of my outfit. I hadn't been surprised by the thoughtful addition. Mark loved to whip my ass until it was striped (just the way I liked it!) but he wasn't cruel. He'd happily dole out all the pain and discomfort I craved but never force me to endure something I didn't need or want.

Mark unsnapped my seatbelt and patted my knees. 'Get up and kneel on the seat. Show me your ass.'

A trill of excitement rippled through me. I did as instructed, putting my hands – paws – on the back of the seat. Back angled just so, I presented my ass to him. He caressed my lower back and smoothed his palm over the leather undies hugging my backside. 'Open your legs,' he urged and nipped at my earlobe.

His fingers dipped under the crotch of the panties, and he quickly found my clit. I gasped at the sudden invasion of his rough fingertips on my tender skin. He cupped my neck with one hand and stimulated me with the other, his fingertips drawing lazy circles around my clit. The tiny pearl swelled with arousal and made my toes curl. He pressed his lips to my ear and whispered filthy promises of what would come after the party. My pussy ached with need and became so wet. His fingers swirled in the slick nectar seeping from my core. He penetrated me slowly and got me so close to coming that I was slapping at the seat and begging him for more.

When he suddenly pulled away and denied me the release I so desperately wanted, I cried out with a strangled 'No!'

Mark swatted my backside and tugged on my ponytail. 'Who owns this pussy?'

'You do, Master,' I replied, fully contrite. 'This is your pussy.'

'Good girl,' he whispered and kissed my cheek. 'And who decides when his little slave comes?'

'Master decides.'

'Exactly.' He caressed my bottom and gave it a playful pat. 'Now hold still while I put in your tail.'

I stifled a groan of frustration. I really, *really* didn't want to wear that thing. He opened the small bag on the centre console and produced the tail and a tube of lubricant. I understood now why he'd gotten me so hot with his fingers. I wasn't like some of the other submissives who ran in our circles. Taking a plug or having anal sex wasn't simply something I could do on command. I needed to be aroused and excited first. Like a good dominant, he made sure my needs were seen to before attempting anything to do with my backdoor.

I moaned as his fingers found the small slit in the back

21

of my leather undies. His wet fingertips traced the pucker hidden there and probed me. I exhaled slowly as his fingers slid inside me, lubing my back passage in preparation for the plug decorated with a puppy dog's tail. I consciously relaxed and pressed back against the silicone plug. It was a bit larger than I was used to, especially for extended wear, but I was determined to work with it.

Mark's other hand slipped inside my undies again. I groaned with pleasure as he strummed my clit and slowly and torturously thrust the tail plug inside my ass. I whimpered as his teeth grazed my shoulder. His fingers moved faster, pushing me closer and closer to an orgasm. I couldn't fight the mounting surge. There would be no holding out and enjoying the gradual build of climax on this one. I howled into the headrest as bliss exploded in my belly and spread through my chest. My pussy pulsed and toes curled as I rocked against Mark's hand, desperate to milk every last ounce of pleasure from his nimble fingers.

'Oh, such a good little slut,' Mark murmured against my cheek before turning my face and capturing my mouth in a demanding kiss. I melted into him, loving the way he called me such dirty names and kissed me until I was breathless. He plundered my mouth, his tongue darting deep inside and swiping mine. I awkwardly clutched at him, those ridiculous paw mittens preventing me from grasping and holding onto him.

When Mark broke our kiss, he swept my bangs from my eyes and smiled at me. 'I know this isn't easy for you, and it's probably going to touch on your fear of humiliation. Actually, I know it is. If you can't handle it, you may use your safe word.' He tipped up my chin and gazed into my eyes. 'I want you to try, all right?'

I nodded and gave him my best imitation of a happy puppy yipping.

He chuckled and pecked my cheek. 'See? You're a natural.'

I didn't respond to that joking remark because I knew I was anything but. I'd embraced the old fake-it-'til-you-make-it mantra on this one. While I enjoyed a variety of kinks and drew very few lines in the sand, humiliation and embarrassment play were on that list of games I didn't want to try. How Mark had talked me into this one was beyond me. He'd been straightforward about tonight's party and had simply requested my attendance as a birthday gift. He swore up and down there was only the touch of a sadist in him but, right now, I was convinced he was the Marquis de Sade incarnate. Asking me to dress up like a puppy and pretend I was a dog as a birthday present? I mean, really!

I hesitantly stepped out of the SUV when he came round to my side and opened the door. My gaze fell to the leather leash and collar clasped in his hand. My cheeks burned with embarrassment as he slipped the collar around my neck, the dog tags jingling against my chest, and clipped the leash onto it. Mark snapped his fingers and pointed to the paved driveway. 'Sit.'

My eyes widened as I realised he wanted me to start playing puppy now, out here in front of our host's house. I nervously glanced around the neighbourhood. It was a gated community and the houses were separated by huge lawns and pine trees. No one else on the street could see me but that didn't lessen my mortification. Swallowing hard, I remembered Mark's request that I give it a try and slowly lowered myself to the pavement. I carefully bent forward until I was on all fours. I kept my back straight and head high. If I had to do this, I was going to be the best damn puppy anyone had ever seen!

I crawled along at Mark's side. I was grateful for the kneepads and mittens. I could just imagine how truly uncomfortable it would have been to crawl from our parked SUV to the door. I kept my eyes down as our host welcomed us into his house. A petite older blonde knelt next to his legs. She wore a diamante collar and seemed suspiciously perky.

When I tried to pass by her, she reached out and nipped my shoulder hard enough to leave a bruise and then growled. Unable to help myself, I yelped and skittered back behind Mark's legs. My arm smarted something fierce. Now this was going a bit too far!

'Mitzi! Bad dog!' The man reached down and swatted

her backside a couple of times. He pointed to a large puppy bed in the corner of the hallway. 'Ten-minute time-out!'

'Sorry about that,' Jake, a man who was known to Mark but not to me, apologised. 'She's having some aggression issues. I think it must be all the lovely young puppies invading her space.'

As Mitzi hung her head and crawled to the corner, I glanced up at Mark and tried to silently communicate what I was thinking: These people are demented! Mark crouched down as an owner might and gently soothed his hand over the bite mark. He pressed a loving kiss to the bruise and stroked my back. 'Would you like to go home?'

I started to answer in the affirmative but then remembered how excited he'd been about this party. I knew how much he loved to push my boundaries, how much pleasure he found in helping me conquer my fears, and shook my head. He grinned broadly, his eyes shining brightly with love for me. He rose and patted my head. 'Come on, girl.'

I crawled next to him, the leash between us loose, and bravely entered the large living room where the rest of the attendees were milling around and talking. I noticed a mix of male and female dominants and puppies. I hoped Mark would keep me at his side like a couple of the others Doms and Dommes did their puppies, but he tugged on my leash and walked me over to a fenced-off puppy play area.

After my run-in with that nut Mitzi, I wasn't so sure about getting close to the other puppies. I crawled into the enclosure and waited for Mark to remove the leash. Before he'd even left, a male puppy nudged a ball my way with his nose. I stared at it for a second, trying to decide if I was really going to degrade myself by pushing a ball around with my nose, and then finally decided that, yes, I was and threw myself fully into the role of puppy.

And it wasn't all that bad. Oh, it was weird all right. It was the most fucking outrageous and bizarre thing I'd ever done in my twenty-eight years. In a strange way, it was oddly freeing and ridiculously fun. I couldn't remember the last time I'd been this silly. Freshman year of college maybe? It had been a long time since I'd indulged the childish playful side of me. Earning a bachelor's degree in three years and a doctorate in four more had pretty much cut out any fun time. It had been nose to the grindstone for so long. I'd never have imagined it would take a fetish puppy party to help me remember what it was like to be silly again.

After twenty minutes or so, our owners collected us from the enclosure and led us into another room. Mark snapped his fingers again and pointed to a spot near his feet. I sat in exactly the way he'd shown me back at the house. We'd practised a bit before leaving. Luckily for Mark, I possessed a nearly eidetic memory so recalling simple commands like 'sit' and 'roll over' was easy for me.

My very own slave

A group of judges walked around and issued commands to each puppy. We rolled over and sat and knelt on all fours so we could be measured and touched and graded like purebred dogs at a kennel show. I wasn't particularly happy with the dog-show portion of the evening but did my very best to show what a good puppy I was for my master. I glanced up at Mark after the judge left me and was happy to see a smile on his face. It was a simple, silly thing, really, but I found so much pride in knowing I'd put that smile there.

When the judging was finished, we puppies were paraded outside into the spacious backyard. My stomach dropped at the sight of the agility course. Mark must have sensed my reluctance because he reached down and lightly scratched behind my ears before stroking my cheek. I thought about dropping my safe word but managed to gather up enough courage to stay in the game.

As I watched other puppies go through the course, most of them awkwardly and slowly and without any agility, I was suddenly very glad of all those Zumba and yoga classes and the off-road races Mark and I ran every year. I might not be the most trained or experienced puppy in the bunch but I could damn sure trot my happy ass around and over that course!

When it was my turn, I crawled at a quick but smooth pace. The tail lodged in my backside felt so strange. It was one thing to wear one during sex or around the house while doing chores but quite another to have it in while I weaved in and out of poles, climbed an A-frame and balanced on a teeter-totter board. I mounted a pause box and performed the commands that Mark gave me with as much finesse as possible. My last obstacle, a long tunnel, gave me flashbacks to a childhood of building forts out of sheets and chairs in the living room with my brothers. Somehow I managed to not make a complete fool of myself and crossed the finish line without being too out of breath.

'Good girl!' Mark crouched down and lightly scratched my neck and rubbed my arms. He pulled something out of his pocket and presented it to me. I almost laughed but then remembered I was still a puppy and opened my mouth instead. Mark placed one of my favourite cherry gummy candies on my tongue. He stroked my head as I enjoyed my treat and watched the last of the puppies go through the course.

Back inside the house, I enjoyed a drink of water from a bowl labelled with my name. I was thirsty enough that I didn't even mind the rather unattractive way I had to bend down and slurp. Mark dabbed at my chin with a paper towel and then led me by the leash back to the living room. I couldn't believe it when I was announced as the winner of the agility course! I'd been sure one of the male puppies had bested me but, apparently, they took off points for certain mistakes.

I beamed as Mark pinned the small blue ribbon on

my leather bra strap. I sat quietly and pressed my cheek to his thigh as other puppies were awarded ribbons for things like best hair and most playful. One of the judges held up a big purple ribbon emblazoned with the words 'Best in Show'. I figured it would go to the male puppy who belonged to the red-haired Domme. He had the look of a Great Dane about him with his muscled shoulders and regal carriage.

'And Best in Show goes to Libby!'

I stiffened with surprise. Mark's hands stilled atop my head. Our gazes met in shock. Finally, he laughed and walked out to grab my ribbon. I preened as he fastened it onto my other bra strap. The weight of the ribbon pulled on the leather but I didn't care. I was pleased as punch with my award. I might not have been the most enthusiastic puppy when I'd arrived, but I'd made the best of it, embracing the experience as something new and different, and look at what that attitude had earned me! Best in show!

After the excitement of the award portion, most of the masters led their puppies back into the living room where they sat around and chatted. I rested on the floor next to Mark's feet while he talked to one of the other Doms, a fellow cop, about police stuff that didn't interest me. I noticed some groups and couples disappearing to other rooms. Soon noises reached my ears that confirmed my suspicions.

'You and your puppy want to join Molly and me in one of Jake's rooms?' Mark's friend cupped his puppy's breast and gave it a squeeze.

I glanced up at Mark to see what he was thinking. One look at his face and I realised I shouldn't have worried. He enjoyed nudging my boundaries but knew that group sex and party sex were entirely off the table. I was willing to dress up like a puppy and prance around an agility course but I wasn't about to let a stranger fuck me. 'I think we'll head on home. My puppy has had a long day. She needs her rest.'

Relieved by Mark's answer, I patiently trotted alongside him as he made our excuses and said goodbye to the dominants still hanging around the living room. We made our way to his SUV, me still crawling and him leading me around by the leash. When we reached the car, he had me stand up and lean against the car with my breasts pushed against the glass. He framed my back, his body curved to mine, and carefully removed the tail plug. I groaned as it finally gave way. The aching sensation of emptiness left me panting. Mark spun me around and grasped my chin in his big paw. He captured my lips and stabbed his tongue inside my mouth. Our tongues duelled as we shared a passionate, lust-filled embrace in the driveway.

'Take me home,' I begged, my body vibrating with need. 'Take me home and fuck me, Master. Be rough with me.' I bit down hard on his earlobe, loving the startled hiss that escaped his lips. 'Own me.'

Growling, Mark separated from me and jerked open the passenger door. He shoved me onto the seat, reached for the seatbelt and buckled me in quickly before slamming the door. He slid into the driver's seat, fastened his seatbelt and left the driveway. On the ride home, his rough, hot hand roamed my exposed skin. He pinched and caressed in a bid to keep me aroused and teetering on the verge of losing it. When we hit our driveway, I could barely contain my eagerness. I wanted Mark so badly it hurt.

We barely made it inside the house. I dropped to my knees when we reached the kitchen and pushed Mark back against the refrigerator. I reached for the front of his pants and grunted with frustration when I remembered I was still wearing those damn mittens. Mark quickly unfastened them and tugged them free. I stretched my fingers a few times before grasping the button of his pants and pulling down the zipper.

I freed his cock for my pleasure and stroked his rigid length. He had a truly magnificent dick. Thick, long and always hard. He had such amazing stamina and control. Lasting power was never an issue. Some nights I'd ride him until I thought I'd just die from sheer pleasure.

I licked my lips and let a little saliva pool on the tip of my tongue before wrapping my mouth around the head of his cock. I slicked his skin with my wet lips and tongue, swallowing all of him on the first go and using those hard-earned deep-throating skills. He groaned and cupped the back of my head. A frisson of delight tore through me. I just loved it when he took control during blowjobs, guiding my head and mouth in the rhythm he loved best. Fast and shallow, then slow and deep, he thrust his cock into my willing mouth. I thought for a moment he would come against my tongue, but he pulled back rather unexpectedly and gazed down at me, his eyes dark with hunger and lust.

'Take off your panties,' he ordered. 'Face down on the tile. Show Master his cunt.'

I trembled with anticipation as I slipped out of my leather undies and got into the position he wanted. I reached between my spread thighs and opened the wet petals of my sex to his inspection. My cheek rested against the tile but my knees were still cushioned by the pads Mark had given me.

'So wet and pink and pretty just for me,' Mark murmured as he knelt behind me. He drew his cock between my silken folds and circled my clit with the blunt tip. I moaned at the wild sensation of his dick stimulating me. He chuckled with amusement and pulled his cock through my pussy lips again. I shuddered and pushed back against him, so desperate for him that I couldn't wait a moment longer.

Mark showed mercy and plunged deep inside me with one powerful thrust. I groaned as he gripped my hips and jackhammered my cunt. There was nothing sweet or gentle about this mating. We were rough and loud and frenzied. My palms squelched against the tile as Mark's thrusts drove me across the floor. My loud cries echoed in the kitchen. Mark panted as he snapped his hips. 'Touch your clit, Libby. Come for me.'

It took only a few flicks of my fingers to send me reeling head first into a powerful climax. I screamed and convulsed as I came so hard I saw stars. Mark's cock continued to stroke my pussy as he chased his own release. 'Libby! Libby! *Libby*!'

Mark slammed deep and shot searing jets of come, claiming and marking me as his. We fell forward on the tile, our bodies still joined, and clutched at one another. Mark's lips ghosted over my ear. Still breathing hard, he whispered, 'I was so proud of you. I wanted you to see that it's all right to be embarrassed and uncomfortable and that sometimes it's perfectly fine to be really silly.' He squeezed my ass and kissed my shoulder. 'And you did.'

'You know –' I drew my initials on his forearm '– you could have just told me that and we could have skipped the puppy show.'

'And miss out on these nifty little ribbons?' He flicked the awards still pinned to my bra. 'Never!'

I snorted and turned my head so I could kiss his cheek.

'I love you, Mark. Even when you're overbearing and demanding and make me dress up like a puppy.'

'I know,' he replied contentedly.

'Happy birthday, baby.'

He grinned and turned my face towards his. My eyelids drifted together as he kissed me. Oh, sure, I was dressed up in the most ridiculous outfit ever, and yeah, my ass was still kind of sore from that stupid tail, but it had been an interesting night. More importantly, I'd made Mark happy. In the end, there were few things I wouldn't do for love.

Seventeen Brass Circles
Sommer Marsden

'What kind of party?' I find myself fidgeting with the hem of my dress.

Something Samuel doesn't like. There are fidgets that are approved and those that are not. The hem thing – a favourite of mine – is unladylike in his eyes. *If you're going to dress like a lady, act like a lady. If you're going to dress like a whore, act like a whore ...*

Which brings me to the worry that is filling me.

He eyes me in the mirror as he fixes his tie. He's to go to dinner tonight with a big client. He's left it up to me if I want to go. After all, it's Thursday. I'm not in his control until tomorrow, despite my urges sometimes. I often find myself wishing Friday would come so I can be his slave. I like to be under his thumb, on his To-Do list ... in his bed.

I shake off my worry and smooth down my hem. He

nods appreciatively before finally speaking. 'It's the kind of party you fear.' Then he grins and it's wicked.

We have our arrangement. I love him and he loves me and Monday through Thursday I am my own woman. Often considered domineering by the men I work with. Some might even call me a ball buster. But I shuck all that when I come through our front door and we are alone. I cater to him, crawl to him, let him make decisions and, yes, he is kind. He treats me for the most part in a way that makes me sigh wistfully for Friday to come.

But this kind of party he's proposing ... that is what I dread. Where the masters parade their pets around. Where the Doms make a Best in Show situation of their subs. My fingers are trembling so I press them firmly to my knees.

'And you want us to go?'

He cocks an eyebrow. 'It's on a Saturday evening. We *will* go.'

I nod, the tremble in my throat threatening to make me cry. *We will go ...*

Images of girls in cat ears wearing belled collars rush through my mind. Dog chains, nipple clamps, crotchless panties, those horrible fetish shoes that are impossible to walk in. Whips and crops and slave bracelets with thin chains that run to hammered metal rings.

I am not flamboyant. I am not showy. I don't want to be put on display.

But … I have agreed. *We* have agreed. And the weekends have become a safe haven for me. A place to surrender and just be. And I cherish it. I don't want to argue over one little party. I don't want to risk what we've carefully shaped. Together.

Because despite the games and the sex and the back and forth … I love him and he loves me.

'We will,' I say, nodding. 'Of course.'

'And tonight?'

I inhale deeply, full of anxiety. I just wish …

He plucks the thought from my head, moving in and unzipping his pants as he does. He pulls his cock free and presses the glans, silken-smooth and warm, to my lower lip. 'If you need to, Paige, we can pretend it's Friday.'

I can only nod as he wedges himself more, filling my mouth, and I moan. I want this. To be full of him. My body, my mind, my soul. I want to not think and just feel. I suck and lick and lap at him until he grunts. That grunt that makes my neck rise up, my skin pebbled. He grabs me by my upper arms, pulls me upright and spins me towards the wall. I'm no fool – I put my arms out fast and brace myself. Spread my legs and put my ass up.

Assume the position.

Samuel is unkind to my panties – tugging and when they snag ripping them up one side. They're gone for good, that pretty pink pair, but then he's in me after sliding his hot flesh along my damp slit hard enough to

37

make me tremble. He moves in me, shoving high and hard, almost lifting my feet off the floor. My toes perch precariously on the cool tile but he holds me firm as he rocks into me. He's watching us in the vanity mirror and I do too. My dress shoved up around my hips, my ass bare above my thigh-high stockings. His cock slipping in and out of me at his will. Two twin splotches of bright red adorn my cheeks. My lips look freshly kissed. My eyes blue and startled. I feel the most beautiful when he's in me and I'm giving myself over to him.

I come. Just from looking at us in that shiny reflective surface.

He chuckles, lips to the back of my neck, fingers pinching my hard nipple through my dress. 'Good thing you weren't supposed to wait for permission, little girl. What do you say, Paige? Shall we pretend it's Friday?'

I nod and push my bottom back towards him. I arch and do my best to meet his eager thrusts and give him what he wants. He grunts again and I tremble. His fingers dig into my hips, his body ramming into me so hard I push my cheek to the wall.

'Yes, sir,' I answer.

Another grunt and as a reward he reaches under the sagging front of my dress and finds my clit. He pinches me repeatedly in time with his driving beat and, when it's all too much and his lips are a thin line of concentration, he rubs me gently as he moves. And that is when my body

– all amped up and utterly confused – capitulates and I come. He's coming with me, teeth clamped to my earlobe to introduce that sparkling bit of pain I usually need.

'Good girl. Go get dressed. I don't want us to be late.'

He pats my ass and smoothes my dress and I move slowly – floaty like I'm dreaming – to do just that. I am much calmer and once again staggered by how much I love this man. I'm half stunned, body thumping with the after-pleasure of him taking me that way.

Finally, he walks in, chuckles and says, 'This one.'

Red wrap dress, black stacked heels, new panties and hair up. That's how I was dressed for our big night out.

* * *

'So are you going?' The man – the client, name of Roker – addresses me and I feel my mouth open and close. Open and close.

Samuel's hand finds my thigh beneath the tablecloth and he squeezes. I shut my mouth and wait. Silent. Smiling, though, so as to make a good impression. Roker's girlfriend is a bottle blonde with inflated boobs, big green eyes and a cotton-candy-pink dress. She drinks her fruity drink like she's making out with it. But she does smile at me when I glance at her, and it's a genuine smile, too. Some women can be catty. This one is not. She's just colourful.

'We're thinking of attending,' Samuel says, moving his hands so our waiter can set down our food. Ribeye for him, crab-stuffed shrimp for me. I have no appetite because all I can think of is my face pressed to the bathroom wall as he fucks me. And that it's Thursday but we are going to pretend it's Friday. The fact that he's told me I'm attending this slave party is haunting me, too.

A vision of myself dressed like a mix of pirate and whore in bondage gear shimmers in my mind and makes me swallow hard. There is a small click in my throat. Samuel, reading my mind, smiles as if amused and squeezes my thigh again. But higher up this time so his pinky finger brushes my mound. A sizzle of arousal skitters under my skin and I'm instantly wet. For him.

'You really should come. It's fun.' Roker reaches out and touches my hand. I feel like a snake has slithered over my skin.

Samuel puts his hand on Roker's, moving it. 'Let's talk business tonight,' he says. 'We can show off our ladies later.'

Even this ballsy, bloated, red-faced business mogul capitulates to Samuel. He nods and they start to discuss supply and demand and shipments and I zone out. But not all the way out, because, as I pick at my food and chat with the Barbie wannabe, Samuel's hand is firmly at the top of my thigh. He squeezes and my cunt flexes for him. There will be more when we get home. More for us. For now, I just have to hang tight.

Finally, he's whisking me out. Getting me in the car. Taking me home. I breathe a sigh of relief.

'I was very proud of you tonight, Paige.' He murmurs this against my neck as we move through our front door into our dark house.

'Thank you.' My voice is breathy and weak. He's touching me.

Samuel nods and the ambient light from outside illuminates only half his face. He looks like a comic-book hero in this light. My stomach buzzes with want, but I don't know what he'll give me. Just teasing and then bed or an actual reward? He puts my hand on his cock and I sigh. Curling my fingers to the long hard line of his shaft, I hear them whisper on the charcoal grey of his slacks. He's shoving my dress up and when he says, 'Hands up,' I obey. My hands shoot into the air and my dress is whisked free, the silken fabric briefly battering my head and hair as he tugs.

'Take those off,' he says in a voice that is a growl and he sets about removing his trousers. Folding them. Putting them on the reading chair.

My fingers shake as I remove my bra, my panties, my hosiery. When he grabs me and reels me in, I give a small cry of surprise and that makes him laugh. His kiss is eager and warm. 'On your knees, pretty girl.'

I drop quickly and take him greedily into my mouth. I love to suck his cock. I love the smell of him and the

41

utterly sensual feel of that skin. I love the way he holds my head and moves me just as he likes and I love that sound he makes when I tongue the tip of him and make him restless.

He only fucks my mouth a little bit, because he's talking when he does. 'I like how you handled that moron. And I like how you managed to keep your cool. I even like how you managed to engage Brenda,' he said.

Her name was Brittany, but I say nothing, licking up the back of his shaft to hear him breathe like a locomotive.

His fingers feather through my hair and he tugs just hard enough to let me know I'm supposed to stand. We are pretending this is the weekend. And on the weekend I do as I'm told. My stomach tumbles with excitement and satisfaction. And, yes, a shining slice of peace has taken up residence in my heart.

'And I like,' he says, moving me back to the sofa and gently pushing me with tented fingers so I drop to the big overstuffed cushions, 'that you didn't just correct me when I called her by the wrong name.'

A small test. I had passed. A blush of satisfaction heats my cheeks.

'Spread your legs.'

He doesn't have to tell me twice.

When he says, 'Don't come unless I say you can,' I feel that familiar urgent anxiety. What if I come by accident? What if I can't control it? He's very good at –

The thought breaks off because he's latched his sweet hot mouth onto my pussy and he's eating me. His fingers smoothing shivery lines down my inner thighs. His tongue, rigid and seeking, probes my swollen clit and I try to keep my breath from running away in my lungs.

'You're very wet.' His fingers plunge into me and he shoves them high and curls them so all the sweetest spots inside of me receive attention.

'For you, sir,' I manage. It's true and I want to say it. I haven't been told I may speak, but I haven't been told I cannot. I take the chance.

It's in my favour because he grunts once and puts his tongue back on me. Maddening, blissful slick circles on my clitoris. Fingers fucking me until the tension in my legs and my back and my arms is almost unbearable. I am trembling to keep myself in check and he whispers, 'You may come, Paige, because you're humbling me tonight. *I* really need to fuck you and I don't want to wait.'

His choice of 'need' instead of 'want' smacks me in the chest and forces the air out of me. I think I'm crying and laughing when I come. All I know is it's hard enough, my sugary release, to bring sparkling fairy lights into my vision. The room is dark but for a second, as my body fires off hormones and pleasure, I see what angels must see.

He moves me the way he wants me. Knees on the

cushions and belly to the back of the sofa. He's in me in an instant, ramming home so that the air rushes out of me and I press my forehead to the wall. 'You may,' he says, reading my mind.

'Thank you.' And I'm tickling my fingers over my still thumping clit as he fucks me. I like to come with him and, when he allows it, it is perfect.

Samuel grips my hips so my skin sings. I will have marks there. I want marks there. When he leans in a bit and presses his cheek to the spot between my shoulder blades, thrusting in sharp, short bursts, I feel the heat of him. And know he's close.

When he says my name, short and fast, just like any other man would, not necessarily a master, but a man who loves a woman, I lose my control. I come with him and there is no reprimand. Only a brief chaste kiss at the base of my neck.

'Shower and then come to bed,' he says.

In bed there will be four black restraints. Because we're pretending it's Friday. We're starting the weekend early.

* * *

Saturday is chilly and he has me sitting in the house wearing silk pyjamas he got me. Nothing underneath. Just me – smooth and perfumed. Every so often, as the day ticks away maddeningly slowly, he lets the temperature

in the house drop. My nipples peak against the soft peri-
winkle fabric and he takes his time, as he talks to me, to
pinch and twist and torture them. By the time twilight
comes, I'm a mess on the inside. Aroused, unfulfilled, my
breasts aching with every beat of my heart.

'Come on now. It's time to get ready.'

I've showered. My hair is clean and curled and done
the way he likes. Up but a bit messy, so he can bury his
fingers in it and move my head or watch me suck his
dick. Small pieces the colour of honey brush the sides of
my face, glowing in my peripheral vision.

I walk up the steps like I have on lead shoes. I don't
want to see what kind of dog-and-pony-show ensemble
he's got me. Nightmare visions of fishnet or Lycra. I am
not a show-off slave. I never thought he was a show-off
master. I guess even people you love can surprise you.
This party is strictly a meet-and-greet of like-minded
folks. And it is all about showing off your pet, slave, sub,
pony girl (or boy) or what have you. There will be some
women with their pretty submissive boys. But mostly it
will be the men. Often they are dressed like leather bikers,
bad asses, very cliché. But others, like Samuel, will be in
subtle, understated but incredibly tasteful suits.

'I bought you something,' he says as I finally clear
the doorway.

I'm not sure if it's relief or just emotional exhaustion,
but when he holds it up I exhale loudly and my knees go

45

weak. He nods towards the bed to show I have permission to sit. I drop like a stone – knees knocking, lips numb. Thank God.

Samuel chuckles softly. 'Come on, doll baby, did you think I was going to prance you around like my prize tart?'

I had hoped not, prayed not; deep down I had not been able to wrap my head around him doing so, but, yes, there had been fear. But I lie to him – taking a risk, I am – and shake my head in the negative.

I eye the gorgeous dress he's bought me. A taupe number with a crossover bodice. I'll be showing off enough – a sample, if you will – but not enough to embarrass me. I am fairly modest. Samuel knows it. The waist is tucked so it will fit me well, the skirt flared but not an exaggerated amount. It will move with me but not twirl out like I'm at a sock hop. There are ivory-coloured thigh-highs on the bed along with a garter belt. No panties. No bra. And a belt.

He sees me eyeing it and smiles. His lips are luscious. When he smiles that way I want to kiss him. Or have him kiss me … everywhere. Plump and full and the perfect shade of pink, Samuel's lips make me think dirty, dirty things.

'This is your lead,' he says.

I blink. My lead? And then I get it. I've seen the garishly made-up women with their dog collars and chains. Even some being pranced around with fine chains attached to pierced nipples. I've seen ponytails jutting from between firm, plump buttocks (both male and female). I've seen the faces of those wearing them, being forced to focus and entertain while stuffed with those anal plugs. The thought is both arousing and horrible to me and I feel hot in the face.

'I think it's a bit much for me to lead a gorgeous creature like you around with a dog chain.' He wrinkles his nose. 'But there must be some sort of ... showing. An honouring gesture.'

'Of course!' I say. The very fact that he might think I'd refuse him his right to lead me around is upsetting.

He chuckles again and leans in to kiss my hair. 'Seventeen brass circles,' he says. 'The tighter I make it, the closer you stay. If I loosen it, you may wander some. If you disobey me, it goes on the tightest notch and there will be consequences.' He runs the belt through his hands: a collection of small brass circles with a fine chain at the end for extension should the wearer need more room. It is a normal fashion belt, not some BDSM trinket. He probably bought it to go with the dress; he might have even had help from some young flirtatious sales girl and it had pleased him. I don't care. I'm just glad I'm not going to be on some dog leash with a ring through my nose.

'You're thinking snobby thoughts about our brethren,' he says, eyeing me.

I lower my eyes. 'Sorry.'

'It's OK,' he says. 'I think them sometimes too. Now get dressed quickly so we're not late.'

We're not late. The place is a large ballroom that one of the members rented out. And my worst fears have come true. There is a girl whose nipples are poking through a sheer neon lime-green top. Her nipples are pierced and two thin chain leads are attached to her body. There is a boy, crawling on all fours by his mistress. He's beautiful – blue-black hair, big brown eyes and a ball gag in his mouth.

I find it all very erotic. My insides quiver at the humiliation and the shame. But I cannot help but feel a rush of anxiety at thinking of my master ever doing that to me. I am utterly relieved and supremely grateful to him in that moment and I press up against him as fully as I can. His big hand is tucked into one of the brass rings of my belt and he says softly in my ear, 'It's OK. Take a deep breath.'

I obey.

A man is rushing towards us. A giant of a man who must easily be six foot six. He has thinning blond hair and water-blue eyes. He's leading a small, dark-haired woman along by a thick leather leash. She smiles at me, looking momentarily confused at my outfit, until she sees the proprietary hand at the small of my back. I can see it in her eyes when she gets it.

Before they actually reach us, Samuel leans in and says, 'Let me handle him. I know you have a temper.'

I almost smile. He's right. When it is not the weekend, I wield my power over an office full of people. I tolerate a lot of things, but stupidity and laziness aren't among them. There are other pet peeves and this man must possess some quality that's garnered me this warning.

'Samuel King, as I live and breathe.' He sticks out his big hand but his eyes are on me the whole time. His little pet is watching, smiling at whatever look must be on my face. The man is huge but he also has a huge personality. Not necessarily one that I like. I can feel it radiating off him in waves. He thinks he's the be-all and end-all.

I already hate him.

'Ned. How are things?'

'Good, good,' Ned says and, to accentuate, he yanks the leash on his girl so her head jerks.

I feel Samuel's fingers curl more tightly on the brass circle – *stay with me*, it says. I can see in his face that he doesn't like Ned's behaviour either.

Ned jerks her hard enough to make her stumble. 'This is my current. Doreen. Turn around, Doreen,' he says. She turns dutifully and Ned smacks her fishnet-clad ass so it jiggles. 'Fucks like a dream,' Ned says as if he's describing a car.

I bite my tongue. Literally.

'And this must be your new –'

'This is Paige,' Samuel interrupts, not moving his fingers from the brass ring of my belt even a bit.

'Ah, Paige,' Ned says and reaches out to stroke my neck. His hand moving decidedly towards my breast.

I don't think, I hiss. 'Stop touching me.'

Ned straightens up fast. His lips press together. His tethered woman blinks and blinks but then I catch a fast and feline smile from her. My face is hot, my heart is pounding because I can feel the tension in Samuel. He tugs the belt and I move up against him again, my ears muffled from my pulse and apprehension.

'Go wait in our tent,' he says.

But he does not loosen my belt. I am to walk directly to our 'tent', one of the draped areas set up for most of the heavy hitters at the function. The ones who ponied up the most money, I guess. Inside each tent is a settee, two chairs ripe for bondage scenarios, a stool and a table set with wine, champagne, glasses and fruit.

I walk away on feet that feel far, far away, toddling a little due to anxiety. The tent that is ours is done up with a cobalt-blue curtain with *S. King* pinned to the fabric. I slip inside and wish I was allowed to pull the curtain shut so no one could see. But I haven't been told to. I sit on the settee, back straight, ankles crossed, knees knocking. From the tent next to us – whose curtains *are* drawn – come the sounds of a good and thorough spanking.

I feel the clench of my pussy and the thump of my

need. God, how I want that right now. That would snap me out of it – it would be penance and pleasure.

'I told you to let me handle it,' Samuel says and I jump. I didn't hear him slip inside. I was far away in the sounds of punishment.

'I'm sorry.' I hang my head and wait. But I hear her receive another blow and hear the sound of her pain but then her subtle moan, and I start to tremble a little.

'He's a pig, but I had that,' Samuel says sternly, letting our curtain drop.

'I'm sorry.'

'Sorry what?'

'Sorry, sir!' I say. How did I forget that? Another spank from next to us and my eyes dart that way. I catch Samuel looking at me and avert my eyes again, press my knees together. I can feel my wetness sliding free of me. I worry about my beautiful dress and punishment and all that jazz.

I worry a lot.

'You disobeyed me.'

I nod and say nothing until he demands I look at him. Then I look at him, eyes pricking with tears. I should have trusted him to protect me. I know Samuel, he does not suffer fools gladly. But the Paige I am Monday through Thursday rose up and yelled above the Paige of Friday, Saturday and Sunday who surrenders.

'What do you have to say for yourself?'

'I loathed him.' My voice is clogged. I force myself to sit up straighter. 'But that is no excuse, sir. I know better. You would have handled it.'

'Because?' He cocks an eyebrow.

Another blow, another cry, another hushed pause from the tent next to us.

'Because you always protect me,' I whisper, feeling my plump nether lips grow slicker still.

'Except?' Samuel prompts, coming towards me, touching my lip with his thumb, popping my mouth open.

'Except sometimes from yourself,' I say. 'Sir.'

He nods. 'Good. Now get your belly over that stool and flip up your pretty little dress.'

'I –' I press my lips together and nod. Doing as I'm told, awkwardly getting on my hands and knees, the stool brushing my belly to help me keep good form. He sits in one of the low-slung chairs. His hand is warm as he strokes me, plucking my garters once. I always fall for it, too. I get lulled by that warm broad hand. Until it bites me and I jump. My cries as he spanks me mimic my invisible sister in punishment next door. I jump some but hold myself as steady as I can. I deserve this. I was wrong and I am utterly sorry. That man made me lose myself and forget Samuel.

When blow ten hits, I am crying. My ass is singing grand opera and blood thumps merrily under my skin, reminding me that I am human and that pain is a very real thing. He pauses, leans forward, puts a finger in my pussy. I cry harder because that is all I want and I know, before I can enjoy it, it will be gone.

And it is, so that five more blows can be slammed down on my welted bottom. He grunts once and my blood leaps. I know that sound. My head is full of the sound of his zipper and he says, 'Turn this way.'

I turn and brush my cheek against his slacks. I nuzzle him and run my face along the soft fabric and his warm cock. My tears are leaving dark marks on the fabric and baptising his flesh. He puts the tip of himself in my mouth and I do what I love to do. I suck him until he pushes his hand into my cleverly mussed hair and guides me.

'Not too much. Just enough,' he says. So I go slow, dragging my lips along his cock. I tongue the tip of him, tasting the perfect saltiness of that drop of pre-come.

'I'm sorry,' I whisper against him, though I haven't been told to speak.

He allows it. Goes soft on me and brushes my bangs back. 'He scared you, didn't he?'

I simply nod. That's that. I have no other words. He knows me.

'Come up here.'

He pats his lap and I rise, my soft dress sliding down over my tender pounding skin. He guides me so that I'm straddling him and, when he brushes his glans along my soaked slit and nods, I sink down, all the breath rushing out of me. There's no room for that air in me, I'm so full of happiness.

I moan. I've been in a constant state of chaotic arousal all day and now he's filling me and moving just so, knowing the rhythm our bodies crave. He pumps up into me and I drive myself down, holding his shoulders in my trembling hands. Samuel grips me hard, yanking me down even as he thrusts up, until I'm making tiny desperate noises.

'You may come when you're ready, Paige,' he says and kisses me.

The kiss does me in. It's sweet and angry and all-consuming.

I come. Three more hard thrusts and he comes, spilling into me, his lips in my hair.

I pull back, looking shyly at him. When he nods, I go ahead and speak.

'Why?'

'Why what?' He tugs one of the brass rings of my belt playfully. He never even had a chance to loosen it and let me roam.

'Why did you give me ... that?' The spanking, the fuck, the orgasm is what I mean.

'Because any good master should be able to see naked need in his charge. And he should have a good enough heart to give her what she truly requires.'

'I love you.'

He nods. I feel the belt go slack and he kisses me. 'I love you too, but don't ruin my reputation tonight, Paige. I'm going to let you mingle. But remember, I'm watching and I'll take care of you. Understand?'

'Yes, sir.'

'Good girl. I think I'd like a wine, Paige.'

He parts the curtains and I find my way to the bar among the brightly festooned guests who are pierced and painted and tethered. They can't quite figure me out, but that only makes me smile as my belt jingles merrily. Seventeen brass circles singing around my waist.

I Am
Charlotte Stein

On the first day, he's cocky and confident, full of vim. He kisses me on the cheek over breakfast, and mentions something interesting from his newspaper. Life is good, he thinks. Happiness is still total. How safe we feel, at moments like these.

But of course by day three the cracks are starting to show. There's no kiss for me over breakfast, and he can't seem to concentrate on his newspaper long enough to share a tidbit.

He's biting his nails again, I see.

And by day seven, they're down to the quick. 'Look at the mess I'm making,' he says to me. 'Look at what you're doing to me.'

But of course it's not really what I'm doing to him at all. He was the one who wanted this. He named the number of days, face as pink and excited as a sex organ I didn't know he possessed.

'Thirty,' he'd said, and after he'd named the number he'd listed the possible tricks he'd use to wheedle out of it. 'Guilt,' he'd said. 'I'll try to guilt you.'

And bitten nails definitely count as such. They count so much I almost waver, but at the last second I remember. I fold the paper I've started reading, and cross my legs in the way he used to do, back when he was strong and brave and still himself. And then I tell him, 'I'm sure you can weather a little tension.' In a way that suggests I've learned my lessons well.

'Don't show me any mercy,' he'd said. 'Be glacial, be aloof. Make me believe it.' And I think I'm getting there, I really do. His face sinks and those bitten fingers drop to his sides, as though he's already abandoned all hope.

I'm the keeper of such things now. I am in charge of what he thinks and feels, and by day nineteen what he's thinking and feeling seems to centre around a kind of tremulous desperation.

I see him going about his usual tasks – shaving, eating dinner, preparing for work – but it's like he's a different person doing them all. Someone else has taken over his insides, and, though he can smile and nod and play the part of a normal guy, he no longer really is.

He's *mine*. He's my raw, trembling creature. He can't move an inch without feeling my cool eyes on him; he can't feel my hand on his shoulder without shuddering. 'Don't,' he tells me, 'don't.'

But it's day twenty-one now. It's time for the next stage of things, just like he asked. 'The first ten days are all about acclimatisation,' he'd said, 'when I'm still fresh and vital and sure of myself. The second set of ten days, I'll start to falter, to wheedle, to beg. I'll test you for cracks.

'And finally … the last ten days.

'Where you test me for cracks.'

And I do. I lie on our bed in barely anything at all, and then I wait, for him to notice all the things he doesn't want to – like the hint of stiff nipple beneath a fold of material, or the glimmer of something that isn't glitter on my inner thigh. They all say in various ways that I'm as aroused as he is, with a few minor differences.

His face is always flushed now. Mine is not. His eyes are glazed, and they claw at me whenever I'm in the same room as him. Whereas my gaze is detached, calm – I swear I barely care.

And, of course, there's one particularly unfair sign that I never have to wear, and he always does.

He's almost constantly hard, now. He goes to work with a stiff cock pushed under something suitably restraining, and comes to bed with the evidence like a fist beneath his pyjamas. I can see it everywhere, all the time – even in the smallest things, like the way he walks.

But he can't have the same from me. He can only tell when I let him, when my arousal will give him the most discomfort, the most cause to break. It's bedtime now, his expression seems to say. Can't we just … can't I just … why are you dressed like that if we can't just …?

But even if I wanted to, I don't think I would, at this point. He could tear the terms of our agreement up right in front of me, say a safe word, beg me to give in … and I'm not even sure it would matter.

I don't want to give in. I'm as lost as he is now. He's buried me deep beneath the causeway of his own desires, and I have no will to dig myself out. 'Please,' he says, 'please,' but he might as well be talking another language.

I'm too far beneath the earth to hear him. Too ready for the next part of the game – the thought of which is almost enough to make me orgasm, all on its own. I simply stand somewhere innocuous – the shower, the break room at work, anywhere at all, really – and the idea comes on me like a thief.

And then steals all of my senses. I'm left breathless before we've even begun, aching in every part of my body. I want you, I think, I want you.

But I don't let him see.

Instead, I change the landscape of the game. It becomes a kind of deception, everything designed to keep the focus on him and away from me. And by the twenty-fifth day I realise just what's happening to the person I thought I was. I was sure I was kind, not cruel. Excitable, not cold.

But it feels cold when I tell him he can no longer wear clothes in the house.

'They interfere with my view,' I tell him, as he looks at me with new eyes. They used to be placid, still eyes, but now they're nothing but fever fever fever all the time. And, though he tries his best to contain that constant shaking, he can't, once he's bare.

He can't contain anything. He can't hide anything.

Just as I can no longer hide anything from myself.

I like the cold, I know. I like it when it scythes its way down my back, as he turns around in front of me – slowly, slowly. It takes him some effort to do it – his legs no longer want to hold him up, it seems – but finally he gets there. He shows me the firm curve of his ass and those shoulders my libido goes mad for, like a model who's been told that *this* is what she's here for.

To be my slut. To be my slave.

'Now what do you want me to do?' he asks, in a voice that is no longer his. He had a deep, sonorous voice, I remember. Now it's like the wind whistling down an empty tunnel. *He's* empty, and he's just waiting for me to fill him up.

'Why don't you go get me a glass of lemonade?' I say, even though that was never part of the deal. 'I want the tease,' he'd told me. 'I want to learn patience.' But this isn't about patience any more.

And I can see that he knows this, by the expression on his face.

He looks like a skydiver on the verge of jumping.

'OK,' he tells me, and this time the whistling isn't quite there. His voice is sturdy, suddenly, and almost the way it was before, as though he's found a new sort of confidence at the bottom of himself.

Unfortunate, really, that my next words strip it away again.

'No, no,' I say. 'Not on your feet.'

And then I wait, until he registers the words and turns, halfway to the kitchen. I watch him freeze in a way that shouldn't thrill me but does anyway. He's mine, you see. He's mine he's mine he's mine, always.

'On your knees.'

'You want me to …'

'I want you to get my lemonade, while on your knees,' I repeat, and I swear for one long moment I'm sure he's going to balk. He does have a safe word – he could use it if he wanted. Or maybe he could just remind me of the terms of our agreement, and point out that there's nothing about knees in there.

He could. In fact, it's so plausible I'm holding my breath over it.

Which only makes his obedience sweeter in the end. I watch him slide down to the floor, and with it goes all of the tension in me, all of the things I'm unsure of. This is how things are now, I see. He's going to crawl to the kitchen and struggle to get me a glass of lemonade, and then I'm going to drink it, while doing something lewd.

61

Like looking at his cock.

Oh, his gorgeous cock. He's so hard, by this point, that it's almost impossible to resist. When he slinks across the floorboards he leaves a trail of pre-come, and even with him on all fours like that I can see it straining towards me. I can make out the swollen head, all glossy and red and just waiting for something good.

A treat, I think, to reward him for his incredible behaviour.

But I don't give him one until the twenty-ninth night. By then he's stopped shaving. He doesn't seem capable of it any more, and he hardly ever speaks – I have to call his work for him, and tell them that he's sick.

While he eyes me in this wild sort of way, as though I've uncovered some new species of animal and let him free in our apartment. He bites, if I get my hand too close, and he growls if I hint at a touch I never actually get around to, and best of all, oh best of all …

He's started coming in his sleep.

The first time he does it, he's mortified – I can tell. I mean, he has almost no shame now. He'll walk around naked for me and pose for me in various undignified positions, and, when I ask him to do worse, he does it without a flicker of resistance. He'll finger his ass now, if I ask him to. He'll soap his body in the shower for my delectation, and kiss my feet at the barest sign that I want him to.

But the first time he spurts into the sheets and all over me … he can't seem to quite process it. His face stays red for the rest of the day, and occasionally I'll see him with his hand over his eyes. I wonder if I'm going too far now.

Until he does it again on the twenty-ninth, all wet and slippery and just ready to be rubbed into every bit of skin I'm exposing. 'Go on,' I tell him, 'go on,' only he doesn't rub the stuff over my nipples, as I expect him to. He doesn't urge the head of his still sticky cock over my belly or my thigh, hoping for more.

He leans down and licks up the mess he's just made instead. Face as red as it was yesterday – but with a different meaning now. He likes the humiliation, clearly. He craves it, in the same way I crave this strange, mute animal I've made, and it's for this that I reward him.

I lick him clean, in return – from the thick base of his cock to the still swollen head, in one long lap. While he turns to stone, on the bed. His mouth makes an O of surprise and his hands make fists at his sides, but none of that is what impresses me.

It's the way he keeps his hips on the bed. I can feel him straining to do it, and I know how much he wants to … but he doesn't. He doesn't do anything but watch, stunned, in a way that nearly sets me alight – though I can't say why.

Until I realise what it reminds me of. That expression

of his; his trembling, near-rigid body; the tentative but rude way I'm licking him ... it's like a sort of mad first time. Somehow we've managed to turn the clock back ten years, and now we're slumped in the backseat of my father's Ford.

And he's gonna get it sooooo *bad*.

* * *

Especially after he's told me, in this sweet sort of wavering tone, 'It's not thirty days yet.'

And he's right. It isn't. But that's not really the point, is it? No, the point is that despite all my idle thoughts about going too far – all of my musings and misgivings, tangling together one after the other – I've actually not gone quite far enough. I'm the one who's holding back. He's the one who's pushing forward.

I want twenty-nine days. He wants thirty.

And, unfortunately for him, I just can't give him that. I have to keep licking his slippery, still stiff cock until he moans for me and lets his eyes close, those thoughts of one more day slipping away from him as easily as a dream. And then, once that's done, it's a short trip to gasping and writhing, to his hands on the very outer edges of my hair – as though he can't quite dare to hold me there.

Not yet. Not yet.

First he has to get permission. He has to wait and see

what the new rules are for something as forbidden as sucking cock. Is he allowed to touch me while I do it? Can he lift his hips when I ease my mouth down over the swollen head of his prick? And more importantly: 'Is it OK for me to come?'

He gasps it out before I've even gotten to the good stuff – that kind of frantic, sloppy suck I love more than anything else – but I don't mind. As much as I love the muteness, it's good to hear him talk. Or beg, if I'm being more honest.

Because that's what he's doing. His lips have set in one long mean line, and I can see him straining against the very thing he's asking for. He's five minutes away from his last orgasm, but he's already on the cusp again, hovering, greedy, ready to spurt whenever I say.

And I've no idea what's more exciting: that he's so quick off the trigger now, or that despite his overwhelming need to shoot he's willing to wait for my permission. He's more than willing to wait, in fact. He's willing to dig his own fingernails into his upper thigh, to stop that feeling from taking over.

Though I don't think such small measures are going to help him for long. He tries biting into his lower lip – hard enough to show red, after a moment – but even that proves useless. He's going to do it and I know it, which is why I suck at him harder. It's why I rub his stiff shaft with one sticky hand, as I make slick circles around and around the head.

I don't want him to bite his lip, you see. I want him to just give in and fill my mouth with hot thick come – and, after a second more, he does. His hips jerk and his glorious groans fill the air, followed by the taste of him, oh that taste I've been missing, all this time.

I won't deny it. I milk him for all he's worth. I keep going long past the point of his satisfaction, and right into the point where he's embarrassed about what he's done and oh so eager to make it up to me.

And that's fine by me. In fact, I think it's a little more than fine. By the time he's between my legs I'm fairly certain I'm shivering all over, in just the way he was only a few days before. And when he pushes his face between my legs, blindly, eagerly, I'm reminded of the way he bit through his own lip.

Because I do it too. I do all the things he did – I moan before I'm supposed to, and writhe beneath the slow, slippery lick of his tongue on my clit – even though I don't have a contract. I didn't agree. I'm meant to be aloof, I think, I'm meant to be cool and collected and not this, not this … anything but this.

I can't be coming already, after barely more than a flick over my stiff little bud. But I am. I can feel it surging up through me, fierce and unchecked, and when it gets to my mouth I scream.

Or at least I try to scream. I try to get out the noise that's been building inside me all of this time, but when it comes to the crunch I'm wordless, soundless … I'm mute. I'm made mute by pleasure so intense it's unbearable. I think I actually fight against it, as though my orgasm is an armed assailant who needs to be put down before he can do worse.

Oh, I've got the feeling there's going to be worse.

After all, I've let it slip now. And I can see it on his face, too, once he's done cleaning my slick folds. Once he's up on his knees over me, smug smile on his too handsome face. He knows, I think. He knows what I haven't, until this very moment.

He's not the slave at all.

I am.

My Night as a Sex Slave
Valerie Grey

Gregory was my lover, although I wouldn't have used that word because it offered the impression he was almost my equal, and I wouldn't have wanted *that*.

Some of our friends teased him about being my little puppy; at that he just smiled, because he had a secret. You see, when I am horny I'm a totally different person; I love being dominated, humiliated and used.

I absolutely *hate* it and I absolutely *love* it.

This has been our dirty little secret: in private I make up for my bitchiness by submitting to him, by playing a game we call 'Fuck Toy'. I'll be his good little slave and do all of his bidding.

When I'm at the height of passion I've always had the fantasy of letting him dominate me in public, but nothing has come of it because once I cool down I am horrified by the idea.

One fateful winter night as we were fondling each other in bed I opened my heart and blurted out the whole thing. He was interested by the idea and we spent hours inventing scenarios. I thought this would be the end of it. But *he* didn't need to be on the verge of an orgasm to be turned on by the idea, and so he kept bringing it up. Eventually, after much insistence and orgasm denial, he managed to convince me. 'Don't worry,' he said, 'I'll plan *every*thing.'

* * *

He had planned a 'private party' in a friend's apartment, and when the time to leave came he had got me really hot and very much into it. The plan was that I'd put on only a dog collar, a leash and one of my long coats, and he'd drive us there with no turning back.

I liked the idea of being totally without any control in public. Just as we were about to leave my apartment I grabbed him painfully by the hair and forced him to look me down in the eyes. 'You *don't* let me chicken out,' I ordered. 'If I try to get out of it you dump me outside naked and leave without me. If you let me get out of this I *swear* you'll regret it.'

This seemed like a good idea at the time; I was hot just thinking about it. Why would I ever want to change my mind?

'Sure,' he assured me. 'I won't let you back out.'

I let go of his hair and he stood back upright. He grabbed the leash that was hanging out of the top of my coat and jerked on it, pulling me stumbling into the hallway. And then he closed the door behind me.

'Follow,' he ordered as he started walking ahead of me, leading me by the leash.

The game had started; I was his little Fuck Toy now. I wasn't supposed to talk unless addressed, and I had to be obedient, among other rules I won't get into right now. I let him lead me down the hall, hanging back just enough so that he'd have to put some pressure on the leash to drag me. I was wearing only a coat that came down to mid-thigh.

This is cool, I thought, starting to wish we'd run into a neighbour. What would happen? What would Gregory 'make' me do?

We got down to ground level and to his car without any incident. Gregory opened his door and moved his seat forward.

'Get in the back,' he ordered.

I was surprised by the request, but did as I was told. He took the opportunity to get his hand under the coat and squeeze one of my ass cheeks as I bent forward to get in and the coat rose up. I quickly sat down in the back seat, looking at him for instructions.

He was still standing outside his door holding his end of the leash. He leaned forward over me, reached for the little handle on the ceiling next to my door window and inserted the leash through it.

He started pulling on his end, shortening my side of the leash, forcing my head up and towards the window until I was sitting upright and had to strain to keep my butt against the seat. He grabbed my wrists and tied them together against the handle, forcing me into that position, my hands above my head.

He patted my bare thigh. 'That's a good Fuck Toy.' His hand crept up my leg until he found my wet pussy. I let out a gasp as he inserted two fingers, massaging my inside. I strained against the leash, scooting my hips forward and spreading my legs to give him better access. He kept playing with me for a little while, then pulled his fingers out and pressed them against my lips. I opened my mouth and sucked hungrily, looking him in the eyes as I did so, teasing his fingers with my tongue.

I was so horny I wanted him to fuck me right there.

We got out of the parking lot and into traffic.

I wasn't in a comfortable position, but I was horny and didn't care; soon enough we'd be at the party and he'd fuck me silly. Then I realised we were not heading for our friend's apartment.

I couldn't tell where he was going. I tried sitting demurely like a good little Fuck Toy, but I was getting impatient and a little anxious; I'd normally be the one in control of the car.

He noticed I was getting agitated, or maybe he'd been checking me all along in the rear-view mirror, and spoke up. 'You're wondering where we're going,' he said. 'I lied to you.'

I felt a chill in my spine.

'The party's not starting at eight; we're not going there – just yet. You think I'd take you there dripping wet? Where's the fun in *that*? No, we'll have a nice little drive while you cool down.'

And drive around we did. It couldn't have been for very long, but it felt like an eternity. My legs were aching from the strain of being just barely sitting, my hands were going numb, I was getting a little cold and I was totally pissed off.

* * *

Our destination: an old duplex. His friend lived on the second floor, with an open-air stairway leading up to his balcony. Gregory opened his door, got out of the car and lowered his seat again, looking at me.

I was starting to have second thoughts about all of this. 'You know I wasn't serious when I –' I began but he interrupted.

'Don't even *think* about begging off, Fuck Slut,' he snapped.

I was so mad at him, and scared too. I didn't know who would be in there.

'Here's how it's going to be,' Gregory said. 'I told them you're a horny little bitch slut cunt whore who wants dirty nasty sex. They didn't really believe me, but they're curious to see what will happen. I also told them to go along with what I say.' He smiled. 'And you don't want me to leave you outside *naked*, right? This is all *your idea*, right? So you *better* go along with what I say. You got that, Fuck Whore?'

I was so pissed off I wanted to choke him with the damn leash.

He untied my hands and I fell back against my seat in relief. I sat there a while, rubbing my hands as the blood started flowing again.

'Give me the coat,' he ordered.

I looked around and didn't see anyone outside. I reluctantly unzipped my coat and handed it to him. He threw it on the front seat.

'Now you're going to come out on all fours and follow me. I don't want to see you at all on two legs tonight. From now on you *do not* talk; you act like a good little doggy would.'

I knew this game; we'd play it sometimes in the bedroom. But I couldn't act like a dog in front of our friends, in public ...

'Please,' I said.

'That's *it*?' he asked. 'If that's how it's going to be, *get out of my car*.'

He grabbed my arm and pulled me out.

'OK! I'll do it!' I said. 'I'm sorry, I'll fucking *do* it!'

He let go of my arm. 'Get out on all fours!' he snapped, taking a step away from the door.

I took a steadying breath, leaned down outside the car and put my hands on the ground. With some effort I managed to get down onto my knees without stumbling. I stood naked on all fours on the sidewalk shaking in shame and felt like throwing up, and to make it worse my breasts were hanging down, pointing at the ground.

I've always been self-conscious about having my breasts hang like that; when I'm horny I think it's obscene and turns me on, but the rest of the time I really hate it.

Gregory tugged on the leash and I moved, the rough ground painful against my knees. When I was out of the way he locked and closed the door. Now there was really no turning back; my coat was in the car. I looked around nervously but couldn't see anyone.

'Come on, slut dog,' he ordered and started walking towards the stairs.

I followed behind as he led me by the leash.

Ever attempt going up a stairway on all fours? There's no graceful way to go about it, especially when you're naked.

I hated the thought that I was exposing my pussy every time I raised a leg, especially as we got close to the top and above ground level where everyone passing through could see me.

We reached the top and I looked around to see if anyone *had* seen me. I couldn't help feeling a little pang of disappointment when I spotted no one.

'Heel!' he commanded when we got to the door.

I did, and sat on my heels.

He knocked on the door and I started shaking again. *This was it.* I waited anxiously and then the door opened. A guy I didn't know stood in the doorway.

'Hi,' he said, looking at Gregory, and then he spotted me sitting on my heels with collar and leash. His eyes nearly popped out in shock. 'And who's *this*?!'

'Oh,' Gregory said offhandedly, 'just a cunt whore I picked up on the way.'

I let out an outraged gasp. How could he *say* that to a stranger? I felt my face flush in shame and anger.

The guy looked down at me in disdain. 'Oh, well, come in. Everyone's in the living room.' He stood out of the way to let us pass.

Gregory took the lead and I followed on all fours, while the guy closed the door. I looked back and caught him staring at my bare-naked ass.

Gregory said, 'Hi, guys! I brought a filthy worthless whore. I hope you guys don't mind.'

They had been sitting around watching TV and drinking beer, and they all turned around and looked at us in surprise. There were four people in the living room: Nigel, the guy this apartment belonged to; Ian, one of

Gregory's friends from work; Ted, a mutual friend from way back, and his girlfriend, Tara. The fifth, the one that had answered the door, was Robert, Nigel's brother.

They all stared at me with expressions ranging from surprise to amusement. Tara just smirked.

I couldn't stand those stares and closed my eyes. I was visibly shaking and close to hyperventilating. Gregory knelt down next to me and started caressing my head. 'Breathe, doggy bitch,' he said. His hand left my head and started caressing my back, then down to my ass. He lingered there a while massaging my cheeks, then down between my thighs towards my pussy. He found my clit and started rubbing it. He leaned close to my head and bit down lightly on my earlobe. 'Relax, slut whore,' he whispered. 'You're going to be just fine.'

I calmed down. I started to forget where I was, my eyes closed and focusing on the sensations in my clit. He removed his hand and I opened my eyes nervously. Everyone had been watching Gregory fondle me.

'Nigel,' Gregory said, offering the leash. 'I need a beer. Why don't you get the Fuck Toy settled in front of the couch …'

'Um, sure,' he said. He got up from the couch, walked around to us and took the proffered leash.

Gregory left the room, heading for the kitchen.

Nigel nervously held my leash and said, 'So, uh, you want to go over to the couch?'

I couldn't reply; I didn't have permission to speak. I looked down at the floor. He gave a tentative tug on the leash and I shuffled towards him, still looking down. He acquired confidence in my demure attitude and led me around towards the front of the couch. Ted and Tara were sitting there, his arm over her shoulders. Nigel sat down next to them, holding my leash. He hadn't given me permission to sit or get comfortable, so I knelt there on all fours directly in front of Ted and Tara. I knew they were getting an eyeful and that shamefully reminded me of my breasts hanging down.

Everyone was still, staring at me. I heard Gregory return. He had two beers in one hand and a bowl in the other. He stood in front of me, set the bowl down, opened a beer and emptied the contents into the bowl.

'Drink,' he commanded.

I lowered my head and started lapping. I knew they were all watching me but this was offset by knowing the alcohol would help settle my nerves. I tried to keep it away, but my hair would sometimes dip down in the bowl. I had to raise my head and shake the hair out of my face before I could resume lapping.

'So how do you like the Fuck Toy?' Gregory asked the observers.

They answered with shy noises.

'Come *on*,' he said. 'She won't bite. You can pet her. Anyone want to *pet* her?'

'Why the hell not?' came Ian's voice, and he knelt next to me. His hands touched my back. I stopped drinking and righted myself on all fours again. He started roaming his hands all over my body. I couldn't help but let out a little shiver of pleasure. I like attention. His hands came down over my stomach and reached my breasts. He grabbed one in each hand and squeezed.

'Make them swing around,' Gregory said. 'She really *likes* that.'

I opened my mouth in protest, then stopped; I couldn't talk. Bitch dogs do not talk.

Ian released my breasts and let them hang, then he pushed them around. 'Like this?' he asked.

'Yeah,' Gregory said. 'She really *loves* that.'

Ian grew bored with my tits and started to explore my pussy. I was very wet, needless to say. My cunt made squishy noises as he fingered it.

'Don't make her come!' Gregory almost yelled. '*No one* let her come. Why don't you make her give you a blowjob? She's really good at sucking dick.'

Finally, things were about to get interesting.

Ian seemed to like the idea. He grabbed my leash, led me to the foot of the La-Z-Boy, fumbled with his trousers and pushed them and his boxers to his ankles, then sat down on the edge of the chair. His cock was average in size and very hard and slick with pre-come. Following Gregory's suggestion he guided my head with the leash, bringing it closer, forcing my mouth to his crotch.

I sat back on my heels; my knees were really hurting. I grabbed his cock in one hand and started licking, cleaning the head of his cock of that pre-come. I took his cock in my mouth. I don't deep-throat, I've got too much of a gag reflex, but I'm pretty nifty with my tongue and lips. Add some ball play with a hand and no man has ever complained.

While I was sucking Ian's cock, Gregory had managed to convince Nigel to fuck me up the ass, something he'd wanted to try but his girlfriend had never gone along.

'Put a condom on so you don't catch anything from the whore,' Gregory said. 'You never know what nasty shit these dirty street bitches are carrying.'

I stiffened at that comment. Ian jerked under me and I quickly relaxed my mouth; good thing he hadn't cried out or I'd have been punished. I was grateful we wouldn't be having unprotected sex, but I didn't like the 'story' at all.

Nigel was behind me and Gregory gave him directions: 'Pump into her pussy a few times, and then put it in her asspipe. Prod her slowly and she'll take it.'

I raised my ass and Nigel got behind me. His cock rested a moment at the entrance of my pussy, and then pushed in. I let out a moan against the cock in my mouth, pushing my pussy against Nigel's cock and meeting him as he pumped, but he quickly pulled out. I next felt his cock against my anus, and tried relaxing my muscles. I had stopped paying attention to the cock in my mouth. I'm used to taking cocks dry in the ass, but it's always uncomfortable at first. Ian grabbed my hair and started fucking himself with my mouth and I went along with the motion.

At first, when Nigel pushed his cock against my asshole, it wouldn't go in and all I felt was pain, but at Gregory's coaching he kept pushing and stopping, pushing and stopping, on and on. He kept at it until the extreme tip of his head started going in, backed off and pushed forward again. This was repeated, penetrating slightly more each time, until the whole head was inside and he gave a powerful lunge and impaled me with his full length. I let out a cry of pain around the cock in my mouth. I was getting off on the pain, though. He quickly pulled out, afraid he'd broken something. I could feel my legs spasm.

'You gotta take it slow at first,' Gregory said, his voice scolding like an impatient tutor. 'You mostly stretched her up now, seeing how her asspipe's gaping. Now just go *slowly*.'

The cock returned to my ass and this time he did as he was told. I was a little sore but I adjusted. He started pumping.

'Stick it in her pussy for lubricant if you have to,' Gregory suggested.

He did: a couple of quick thrusts in my pussy and then

he went back to my asshole. This was much better; he could slide in easier and started fucking me hard.

I knew that soon I wouldn't be able to pay attention to Ian's cock in my mouth, so I attacked it with urgency, giving it everything I had so I could focus on the splendour in my ass.

I felt so *dirty*, like such a *whore*, and I wanted more. I pulled Ian's cock out of my mouth and aimed it at my face, jerking furiously. He came, letting out three big squirts of splooge; one landed on my nose, the second on my upper lip and the third on my chin.

I'm not sure, but I think I had a small orgasm.

I licked the spunk off my upper lip.

Now I could really get into the ass-fucking. I braced myself for support against the La-Z-Boy with one hand, meeting the incoming thrusts halfway as the other hand sneaked to my clit. I only managed to play with it for a couple of seconds before my hand was snatched away.

'*No!*' Gregory said. 'You *don't* get to come yet.'

This wasn't fair; anal sex feels really great but it had never given me an orgasm by itself yet. All I could do was kneel there and take it as spunk dripped down my face. Let them get their fun without getting anything myself. I really was just a Fuck Toy.

I could feel Nigel's thrusts grow in urgency. He started grunting, gave a couple of hard deep thrusts, and then he was immobile in my ass.

'God, that was cool,' he said and pulled out.

I felt a chill of air on my wide-gaping asshole.

'Hey, Robert,' Gregory said. 'Now that your brother's done with her rump, do you want a go at it?'

Nigel was pulling his pants back up, Ted and Tara were half-naked, fondling each other on the couch, Gregory was sitting next to me drinking a beer, and Robert was standing where he had a view of the room; he had his cock out and was stroking it slowly.

Next, they had me lie on my back on the coffee table, my butt hanging just off it. Robert put on a condom and knelt between my legs, then he grabbed them and plunged into my asshole. This was so maddening. Here I was getting ass-fucked again and I couldn't come.

Gregory put his beer down, knelt next to me and started sucking on my breasts and playing with my nipples.

I *needed* to come. This wasn't fucking *funny*.

Robert didn't last long; he'd barely just started and already he was moaning heavily.

'Pull out and come on her stomach,' Gregory told him. 'She likes it when strangers shoot a load on her. *Don't* you?' he said to me.

I nodded.

Robert pumped into my ass a couple more times then pulled out, tore the condom off and stroked himself. The first spurt landed between my breasts, the rest on my belly.

Ted and Tara started having sex on the couch.

Gregory gave me a beer and ordered me to drink it down. I did gratefully. We both sat on the coffee table, me in front and him behind. He teased my breasts and pussy and stopped when I was liking it too much.

The guys were starting to get hard again, watching Ted and Tara go at it. Eventually Ted came, shooting his load into his girlfriend's pussy. They separated, both panting and a little uncomfortable at all the attention.

'Tara,' Gregory said. 'You mind if the Fuck Toy sucks and eats that spunk out of you?'

She sat on the edge of the couch and I knelt between her legs. First I licked the spunk that had started leaking out of her pussy, tasting her boyfriend's splooge, and then I started digging in with my tongue. I cleaned her up, but I was more interested in making her come than eating come. I attacked her clitoris with my mouth like Joan of Arc on the English castle wall. I penetrated her with my fingers like the slut pervert I was.

The guys cheered us on as I ate her out. I could tell she'd never been with a girl before; she started really getting into it, wrapping her legs around my head. She came pretty hard, squirting some pussy juice straight into my mouth.

I sat back, wiping my mouth with my hand.

'Nice,' Gregory said. He lowered his pants and lay back on the coffee table, his dick erect. 'Straddle me. You've got more work to do.'

I climbed on the table and lowered myself on to his dick. I didn't want to play around; I started fucking him hard. He grabbed my breasts and slapped them around like fun bags. We were the centre of attention and I liked it, all of them watching me fuck in a frenzy.

Someone put a finger in my asshole and then made me suck it clean.

I fell down on Gregory. He took me in his arms and turned us around, him now on top and me on the bottom. He went at it for a while, pulled out, grabbed me by the hair and came all over my face.

I self-consciously crossed my arms over my breasts. I felt tears of shame in my eyes and closed them, uncomfortable.

'You want to leave, don't you?' Gregory said.

I nodded.

'But the guys are hard again. Do you want to let them fuck you or do you want them to masturbate and come on you?'

'Masturbate,' I mumbled.

'Don't move. Aim at her face, guys, OK?'

My eyes were closed and I listened to them jerk off near me. I was hit a couple of times on the face with splooge and the next guy did the same. I had to scoop spunk away so I could open my eyes.

I was a mess.

I was a slut.

Fuck Toy.

I looked at the floor, ashamed, spunk dripping all over me. Gregory took the leash, ordered me on all fours again and led me towards the door.

I didn't look back.

He stopped and said, 'Night owls, hope you had fun with the whore. It's the best *fifty bucks* I ever spent.'

I wanted to cry.

He opened the door and led me out. If you think going up the stairs on all fours is hard, just wait until you try going down them. I had to go down backwards, ass first, naked.

He had me sit in the back of the car and tied me again. He didn't let me put my coat on. I had to endure the whole ride back home naked with dried spunk all over my face.

He led me out to my apartment, naked, leaving the coat in his car. I was nervous as hell, but we didn't run into anyone.

We were safely in my apartment and everything was mostly over. I had to admit I was turned on again, thinking about my humiliations that night.

We had sex again as soon as we got inside, right on the floor. He came on my face and refused to let me wash any of it off. I had to go to sleep that way, smelling like a spunk whore.

The next morning, my body ached all over. I had a

sore asshole and caked spunk had dried all over my face, hair and breasts.

I slapped Gregory awake and told him I'd make him pay dearly for last night.

'You fucking *bastard*,' I said.

He smiled.

Minding Rex
Elizabeth Coldwell

'Tracey, you might be asking yourself why I've brought you here.'

Setting down her glass, Tracey wondered what was coming next. She should have been suspicious; for the last three years she'd worked as Mariah Kensit's secretary, and in all that time they'd never once socialised together. Mariah had strict rules about keeping her business and personal relationships separate, and she'd made it very clear to Tracey when she'd first employed her not to expect girls' nights out together, or spa-day treats on her birthday. So, when, as they travelled down in the lift together that evening, her boss had suggested they visit the cocktail bar round the corner from the office, Tracey had been surprised, but she hadn't refused. Now she began to think she should have. It was an open secret that the agency wasn't doing as well as it had been this time last year. Maybe Mariah had brought her here to buy her a drink or two as a prelude to breaking the news that they were letting her go.

She said nothing, simply waited for Mariah to continue.

'I need you to do me a favour.'

That, at least, didn't sound like a polite way of telling her she was to be made redundant and Tracey relaxed a little, sipping at her hazelnut martini.

'I'm going away this weekend,' Mariah went on. 'An old university friend's getting married in Chepstow, and that means I need someone to look after Rex for me, which is where you come in.'

Rex. Mariah often mentioned him, but Tracey paid very little attention. She always imagined some fussy, yappy little breed of dog – a pug or a Bichon Frisé – and she wasn't at all keen on the animals, with all their smell and their mess and their slobbering tongues. 'Oh, I don't know. I'm not very good with pets.'

'Well, you and Rex will get on splendidly, I'm sure of it. I want you to come over to my house tomorrow evening after work, so I can introduce the two of you. And pack an overnight bag. You'll be staying to keep an eye on him.'

Now Tracey's curiosity was piqued. How high maintenance did a dog have to be that it required round-the-clock attention, rather than a simple walk and a bowl of food twice a day? And weren't there more than enough boarding kennels that offered that kind of service? But it indicated the depth of Mariah's trust in her – something she never openly stated in their day-to-day interactions – and, more importantly, it would give her the opportunity to spend time in her boss's home. She certainly wasn't going to pass that up.

'OK, I'll do it.'

'Thank you, Tracey. I knew I could count on you.' Mariah drained the last of her Cosmopolitan and put down enough money to cover the bill and provide a generous tip for the bartender, whose taut black-trousered arse she and Tracey had been admiring all evening. She snatched up her bag and bade her secretary a curt good-night, leaving Tracey to ponder exactly what she'd let herself in for.

* * *

Mariah owned a three-bedroomed terrace house on a quiet street within walking distance of Hampstead Heath. The heavy curtains at the mullioned windows and the potted bay trees by the door didn't scream ostentatious wealth, but Tracey knew just how hard her boss had worked to be able to afford a home in such a desirable neighbourhood. From the stories Tracey had heard whispered around the office, Mariah's stiletto heels had trodden on more than one pretender to her role as head of the talent agency, but, as Mariah herself so often said, being nice got you nowhere in this business.

'Indeed, Tracey, if only you were a little more ruthless …' she'd added on more than one occasion. Tracey had never been able to work out quite what she might achieve, but she suspected it was a step or two up from fetching her boss's lunchtime sandwich and placating some of the agency's more excitable clients when they refused to believe Mariah really was in a meeting.

Tracey rang the doorbell and waited. Mariah had left the office an hour before the agency's usual closing time, explaining that she needed to have everything ready for Tracey's arrival. Despite her uneasy relationship with dogs, Tracey intended to get on with Rex, and she'd nipped out at lunchtime to buy a squeaky rubber toy in the shape of a bone, in the hope of making friends.

The door swung open. 'Ah, Tracey, do come in.' Her boss, resplendent in a smart black coat trimmed with faux fur, ushered Tracey into the house. 'Come through and meet Rex.'

Tracey followed Mariah into the kitchen, clutching the squeaky bone. 'Hey there, Rex!' she called in what she hoped was her most pet-friendly voice, aware of a curled-up shape in a dog basket close to the Aga, considerably larger than the handbag-sized pooch for which she'd mentally prepared herself. 'Come and see what I've got for …'

Her voice trailed off as she registered what actually sat in the basket, head cocked in a mixture of curiosity and fright at the sound of her voice. Not a dog at all, but a man, stark naked but for a wide black leather collar around his neck.

At first, Tracey was convinced she'd been the victim of some sick practical joke. She almost expected the agency's other staff to pop out from under the kitchen table, yelling 'Surprise!' and filming her startled reaction on their smartphones. But something in Mariah's expression told her this was all thoroughly serious.

'Don't be alarmed, boy,' Mariah crooned, running a hand through the man's dark shaggy curls in a gesture that combined love and clear ownership. 'This is Tracey. She'll be looking after you till I get back from Wales.'

The man nodded at Tracey in greeting, but didn't speak. Now she was over the initial shock, she found herself studying him more closely. With his ice-blue eyes, broad, open features and an athletic physique of which she could see rather more than was proper on first meeting, he was as handsome as any of the actors on the agency's books. Indeed, that was very probably how Mariah had first met him; Tracey pictured him coming in for an initial meeting and being asked to demonstrate the kind of talent that wouldn't necessarily land him roles but had made him a fixture in Mariah's bedroom. Or, more accurately, kitchen, if the big tartan dog bed really was where he slept on a regular basis.

'I could have explained before you got here,' Mariah said, breaking off from petting Rex, 'but I knew that either you'd have freaked out and refused to come, or you'd have spread the story of my special pet all round the office.' Mariah took a step towards Tracey and lowered her voice. 'I do hope you realise the risk I've taken by allowing you to see Rex. I've put my trust in you, Tracey, and I really don't want to see that trust abused. I'm sure you understand it would be rather difficult for you to keep your position at the agency if that happened.'

The threat duly noted, Tracey replied, 'But why me? And why aren't you taking Rex to the wedding with you? I mean, he is your boyfriend, isn't he?'

Mariah laughed. 'Oh, Tracey, sweetheart. I can see there's plenty I need to explain here.' She glanced at her watch. 'But there's time before my cab arrives, so ... Yes, Rex is my boyfriend, but he's also my submissive. Think of us as mistress and slave, if that makes it easier for you. And I've gradually trained him up as my pet, simply because that's the role I feel suits him best. And he doesn't complain, do you, boy?'

'No, Mistress.' Rex spoke for the first time since Tracey had arrived, an appealing musical tone to his baritone voice. Somewhere not too far from here, Tracey couldn't help but feel, a West End show was missing his talents.

'And as for the reason why he's not coming to the wedding with me – well, I enjoy cuckolding Rex. You can't imagine how frustrated he gets, knowing I'll be spending the night with another man, giving him everything I deny my disobedient pet. Stand up and show Tracey what I mean, boy.'

At the command, Rex rose from his basket, and for the first time Tracey saw the clear plastic device strapped around his cock, designed to prevent him from getting an erection.

'So you see, while Rex is in enforced chastity, I'll be getting cosy with an old university boyfriend of mine. Mm, I'm looking forward to reacquainting myself with that big hard cock of his ...'

Rex squirmed visibly, while Tracey did her best to understand this most unorthodox arrangement. Obviously it suited them both, or Rex would never stand for it, but she couldn't imagine how it must feel not only to be denied your own pleasure, but also to know your partner had deliberately set out to achieve their own.

'Anyway, I led Rex to believe he'd be on his own and able to look after himself this weekend. Have the run of the house, sleep in a proper bed for once ...' Mariah raised a perfectly threaded eyebrow. 'Wasn't that wicked of me? But I'm sure he'll enjoy you enforcing the kind of discipline he's become used to over the months, won't you, boy?'

'Discipline?'

'Oh, yes. Rex can be a very bad boy, and sometimes he needs to be reminded who's in charge. I recognise a lot of myself in you, Tracey – the same desire to be in control, on top of things at all times – and I think you have the potential to become a strict but loving mistress, to find yourself a man who'll worship and obey you just as Rex does me.'

'Mariah, I'm really not sure –' Was that really how her boss saw her? Tracey had never considered the prospect of dominating anyone until now – because that, she knew, was what Mariah meant – but she couldn't deny that the thought of telling the gorgeous naked man who crouched on the floor before her exactly what to do was a strongly appealing one.

'Nonsense. You'll be fine. I've left a list of when Rex needs to be fed, bathed, walked. It's all perfectly simple. Just make sure he doesn't go on the living room couch.' The doorbell chimed, cutting into Mariah's instructions. 'Oh, that'll be the cab. One last thing,' she added, before leaving the kitchen, 'Rex may try to act up since I'm not around. In which case, discipline him as you feel appropriate. You'll find what you need in the bedside cabinet in the guest bedroom. You'll also find the key to his restrainer there, though I doubt ...'

With that, she was gone, sweeping out to her cab in a cloud of Chanel No. 5. Rex watched her go with something very like devotion on his face.

'Don't worry, she'll be back soon enough,' Tracey assured him, still wondering quite how she'd found herself in her boss's kitchen, in sole charge of a submissive human pet. 'And in the meantime –' she consulted the printed sheet of instructions Mariah had left for her '– it's time for dinner.'

According to Mariah's notes, Rex had already prepared their evening meal, which should be sitting in the fridge, ready to be heated up. When Tracey opened the plastic container labelled 'Friday Night', she found a lamb stew, fragrant with the aroma of red wine and thyme. A tray was already set with a plate, the appropriate cutlery and a wineglass – Rex's doing again, she suspected. His portion was to be served in the stainless-steel bowl that stood by his dog bed.

The remains of the wine he'd used to make the stew stood on the counter, and Tracey poured herself a large glass. Rex looked at her longingly as she drank, but she knew better than to offer wine to a pet. Without even being aware of it, she was already coming to view him as though he was of a lesser order than herself. Maybe Mariah knew her better than she knew herself, guessing that she'd settle with ease into the dominant mindset.

Once she'd heated up the stew, and cut herself a hunk of sourdough bread to accompany it, she spooned some on to the plate. Then she picked up Rex's bowl and put the rest of the stew in it.

'Mistress Mariah likes to have dinner in the living room,' Rex pointed out. 'I can put on the TV for you if you'd like, find something you want to watch.'

Tracey shook her head. 'No, I think I'll eat in here tonight.' Though she didn't say it out loud, she wanted to watch Rex eat from his bowl. She couldn't explain why the thought of it intrigued her so much; all she knew was that her panties were wet just from the thought of seeing him on the floor, gobbling up his food just as a dog would.

'Here you go, boy.' She set the bowl down on the floor, brimming with the rich, aromatic stew, and found the perfect vantage point at the table. Without any self-consciousness, Rex got down and started to lap at the stew. How gorgeous he looked, Tracey thought, naked behind presented to her, his spread thighs offering her the occasional glimpse of his balls, heavy with unshed seed, and restrained cock. She took her time, savouring both the stew and the sight of Rex at his own meal. When she'd finally cleared her plate, and Rex had licked his bowl clean, she asked, 'So what does your mistress do once she's finished eating?'

'She calls me into the living room, and I give her her dessert.'

She knew from the tone of his voice he wasn't referring to food, and her pussy clenched with lust. 'And are you going to give me my dessert?'

There was no hesitation, even though they'd met barely an hour earlier. 'Yes, ma'am.'

Rex crawled over to where she sat, gazing pointedly at the fork of her thighs where it was covered by the loose folds of her summer dress. When she reached up underneath it to remove her panties, he stopped her. That was part of the service he offered his mistress, and so he would do the same for her, pulling the wisp of lace, saturated with her juices, down and off.

For a while, he crouched on his haunches, not moving, simply staring at the treasure hidden between her thighs. She'd never been with a man who'd scrutinised her so intently, or found so much beauty in the soft frills of her pussy lips. By the time he flicked out his tongue to taste her, she was already halfway to orgasm, turned on past the point of endurance simply by having him gaze at her cunt.

Whether he'd come to his mistress/slave relationship with the exquisite oral skills he displayed, or whether Mariah had trained him in the art of eating out a woman, Tracey neither knew nor cared. All that mattered was the feel of his supple tongue-tip playing in slow figures of eight over her clit, and the way he broke off from time to time to take her inner lips into his mouth and suck gently on them. Her fingers twined in his curls, pulling him harder on to her crotch, so that the hard ridge of his nose bone added the extra stimulation she needed to send her tumbling into orgasm.

He didn't stop once she'd come, simply turned his attention to her arsehole, licking her there until he judged she was ready for more pressure on her sensitive clit. She came three times before she finally cried enough, conscious that in all this process he'd been kept frustrated, the cleverly constructed restrainer preventing him from getting the erection that the sight, smell and taste of her would otherwise have had springing up hard and ready. She could get to like this, she thought, as she rose from her chair on legs so weak they could scarcely bear her weight. And she still had the rest of the weekend to discover how much more fun she could have caring for this very special pet.

* * *

Saturday dawned bright, the heat of the day already apparent as Rex prepared tea and toast for Tracey's breakfast. She'd let him sleep on her bed in the guest room – as far as she could see, that wasn't ruled out in Mariah's list of dos and don'ts – and he'd seemed quite happy there. Even so, when she'd woken, it had taken her a moment to remember quite why she had a naked man curled up at her feet.

'We'll be going walkies this morning,' she informed Rex as he poured her a cup of Earl Grey.

Mariah hadn't left her any specific instructions about

walking her pet, and at first she'd thought a few circuits of the big back garden might suffice. Then she remembered the bathing ponds on the Heath, where male nudity was not an unusual sight. She wanted to be seen by others in her role as Rex's temporary mistress, wanted their unspoken approval, and this seemed as good an opportunity as any to make that happen.

He didn't protest when, breakfast things washed and cleared away, she fetched a raincoat from the hall and ordered him to put it on. He looked vaguely ridiculous by the time he'd slipped into a pair of canvas deck shoes and she'd fastened the lead that hung on the same peg as the raincoat around his neck, but she was sure his submissive heart thrilled at the humiliation.

Their route to the park took them down quiet side streets, and Tracey was disappointed that almost no one was around to notice them as they passed by. Only one man gave them a curious, prolonged look as he polished his Mondeo, but she suspected he was the type who twitched his curtains whenever anyone made their way past his front window, his nosiness more force of habit than any serious interest in Rex's bizarre mode of dress.

Once they were on the Heath, she made Rex take off his raincoat and clipped the lead around his neck, fastening it to the D-ring in his dog collar. He looked magnificent, so vulnerable and yet so proudly masculine, and as he trotted along obediently at her heels she preened inwardly, delighted at how readily he'd responded to her domination of him. If this was how it felt to have a slave, she needed to start looking for one of her very own, unless of course Mariah was open to some kind of sharing arrangement.

Swimmers in the male pond paused to watch them as they made a slow circuit of the water's edge. The pond attracted a number of gay men, who used their naked swims as an opportunity to cruise for new lovers, and they paid particular attention to Rex's toned physique and firm arse. Tracey watched their gaze drop to Rex's restrained cock and saw their faces break into broad knowing grins that left Rex blushing furiously, his humiliation complete as they divined the truth of his relationship to the woman who led himYet he was clearly loving the attention, digging in his heels and tugging at his lead when Tracey tried to move him on, acting up like a disobedient puppy. Suddenly, she couldn't wait to be back in Mariah's house, where she had access to the punishment implements her boss had mentioned.

The walk home was swifter, both of them knowing what was on the agenda; Rex just as eager to be punished, it seemed, as she was to punish him. No sooner were they through the door than Tracey was taking the stairs two at a time, dashing into the guest bedroom to retrieve the first tool her fingers closed around – a wide leather belt – and the key to Rex's restrainer.

His joy at having his cock freed from its cruel bondage was short-lived, as she ordered him to bend over and touch his toes. He didn't disobey her, even though he knew exactly what was coming. Never having wielded a belt before, her blows were cautious, but still carried enough force to leave reddened stripes on Rex's arse. Half a dozen would do it, she thought, and, though he took them in relative silence, only the odd whimper escaping from his lips, she must have been hurting him. How well trained he was, to suffer so stoically, and how she longed to see him put through his paces by a mistress more experienced in the art of discipline than she was.

'Bad boy,' she snapped, as the belt landed for the final time. Her hand caressed his arse, feeling the heat in his freshly beaten flesh. 'But you won't do it again, will you?'

He shook his head, looking so contrite that she decided he'd suffered enough.

'Bet you'd like to come now, wouldn't you?' she said, noticing how his cock stood to attention. She gave him just long enough to think she might aid him in the task, then ordered, 'Wank yourself off for me, boy.'

His hand flew to his cock, gripping it and tugging in a swift back-and-forth rhythm, as his other hand rolled his swollen balls. In other circumstances, she might have made him put on a display for her, stretching out his pleasure as long as he could, but he was already past the point of showing any restraint.

'Come for me,' she ordered, and his spunk shot out as if on cue, landing on the marble tiling. 'Now lick that up, you bad boy.'

Rex got down at once, and began to lap at the sticky puddle on the floor, clearly well used to the taste of his own come. Which was the exact moment that the kitchen door swung open and Mariah stepped into the room.

'Well, it certainly looks like you've got the hang of this pet-sitting lark,' she commented, smiling at Tracey's stunned expression. 'Rex, when you've finished cleaning up your mess, I want you to bring Mistress Tracey and me two glasses of champagne in the living room.' She linked an arm into Tracey's, the established mistress welcoming a sister into the fold. It was a gesture that made her think this strange weekend of exploration and domination was far from over, despite Mariah's untimely return.

'We've got plenty to discuss, the pair of us,' Mariah continued. 'Mistress Tracey is going to tell me just how she's disciplined you in my absence, and I'm going to tell her quite how much of a scene you can create by bedding the groom on the eve of his wedding ...'

The Breaking of Sub Paul
Kyoko Church

One red shoe.

That was it. One. Red. High-heeled. Open-toed. High-sheen satin Kate Spade slingback shoe. Perched atop his desk at work.

What did it mean?

He immediately broke out into a sweat. Could it be?

He looked around his office. Nothing else seemed to be out of place. He looked back out the door, up and down the hallway. Nothing or nobody unusual. His personal assistant looked up from his desk in the common area across from his office. 'Looking for something?' he asked.

'No,' he said. 'Actually, yeah, did you see anybody come in my office earlier?'

'Well, I went in and put the notes from the last meeting on –'

'No, I mean, someone else. A woman.'

His assistant smiled a little hesitantly. 'A woman?'

'Yes, a woman, a red –' He looked down and blushed. 'You know, it's nothing. It's probably nothing. Sorry.' He went back in his office and sat down at his desk. He pulled his laptop out of its carrying case. And then he thought: email. Of course.

He opened his mail. And sure enough. There it was.

* * *

His cock was so hard. He couldn't believe how hard it was. And she hadn't even done anything, he hadn't even seen her. Yet.

He had no idea what she had planned or how long she'd be around this time. It must be the memory of what she'd done to him a year ago, the quivering, aching, little mess of a boy she'd reduced him to for those three weeks after he first met her. He hadn't let himself even begin to think of all the humiliating things she put him through. But his cock seemed to have a memory of its own.

So, as he stood there outside her office door on the forty-second floor, with her shoe in his hand, preparing himself to knock, steeling himself at the exhilarating prospect of actually seeing her again, his cock stood at full attention. There was no hiding the shameful bulge.

And then somehow he was there. Kneeling in front of her inside her closed office. He'd barely caught a glimpse of her before he prostrated himself at her feet, as if looking at her would be like looking at the sun, so hot and bright as to be blinding. Her feet were stockinged, and by her desk he spied the mate to the shoe in his hand. Without looking up, he offered the one she'd left him.

She laughed her crystalline laughter that he remembered so well, the laughter that haunted his dreams. 'My prince!' she sighed. 'Well, doesn't this make me feel just like Cinderella. I assume you got my email and are accepting my offer, then?'

He mumbled assent.

'That's not a good beginning, sweetie. Speak clearly for Mistress, please. Has it been so long you've forgotten the importance I place on good manners?'

'I'm sorry, Mistress,' he said, finally looking up at her. Her waves of red hair were even more shiny and beautiful than he remembered them. In his fantasies her hair was always up as it had been when they first met. So this vision of her now, softer, with her red locks framing her sparkling hazel eyes, and full red lips in her astonishingly and exquisitely contrasting pale-skinned face, was mesmerising to him. 'I guess I'm just a little nervous. I didn't think I'd ever get to see you again.'

'Aw, sweet boy. I've missed you too. Why don't we go over to the couch and you can put my shoes back on my feet. I know you'd like that. And then I have a present for you.'

Her feet. Her beautiful, slender, exquisite feet. Holding one in his hand after holding one in his dreams for so long made him yearn to kiss it. He looked up at her. She nodded knowingly. 'One,' she said. So he placed one reverent kiss on the top, as he inhaled her scent, the nylon of her stocking brushing his lips.

The shushing sound of the nylon against her shoe and the subtle pop as her heel slipped into place made his cock ache.

Once her shoes were back on and he was kneeling on the floor in front of where she sat on the couch, she pulled out a box and offered it to him. He reached up to take it but she drew it back slightly.

'Ah, ah, ahh,' she said. 'Not quite so fast. If you read my email thoroughly, I believe you have something to say, something to ask first?'

He swallowed. He concentrated, trying to focus his mind and remember the words he'd prepared. He swallowed again, took a breath and spoke.

'Mistress, I come before you humbly requesting your time, your gifts, your affection, your infinite knowledge about me and my inadequacies and your control. You alone are the person I desire to submit to because you somehow know exactly what I need to learn and you alone have the strength, the compassion, the wisdom to help me learn it. It helps, of course, that you are without a doubt the most beautiful, sexy, alluring woman I've ever known. So I ask that you allow me to submit to you. I pledge to do whatever you say or accept any punishments you deem appropriate.'

By the end of his speech, he could barely breathe. He was shaking. He stayed there at her feet and awaited her response.

'Well, sweetie,' she said, placing a slim finger under his chin and raising his gaze to meet hers. 'That was absolutely lovely. I accept your request. Here is your gift.' And she handed him the box.

His heart hammered in his chest. She was giving him a gift! What could it possibly be?

He opened it and immediately was puzzled. What at first glance appeared to be a watch he could see, after a second, was not.

'I know it doesn't seem so, but it was actually very expensive. It's vintage, you know. They don't seem to make them any more.'

He continued staring. The numbers around the edge going up to 60. The two hands, one bigger and red, the other smaller and black. The two silver buttons on the side.

It was a small stopwatch. With a wrist strap.

His heart pounded harder, although he still wasn't quite sure why. He looked up at her, not knowing what to say.

'Aw, you're confused, aren't you, darling? Well, don't worry. I'll explain it to you.' As she spoke she took the gift out of the box and began strapping it on his left wrist. 'This is your collar. It has two purposes. One is as a visual reminder. Your cock belongs to me. When you see your watch throughout the day, I want you to repeat that in your head. My cock belongs to Mistress. Say it now.'

'My – my cock belongs to Mistress,' he stammered as she finished strapping on the watch.

She turned his wrist over and they both stared at it.

'Very good.' She smiled and continued her explanation. 'The second purpose is with regard to time. Time is your issue, isn't it? Or rather, *timing*. So this stopwatch is perfect. Because your submission will be a lot about timing. As in, timing you.' She pressed the top button. Tiny ticking noises burst from his wrist as the red hand glided smoothly around the dial.

Oh, God. GOD! His face burned bright, the hottest it ever felt. He couldn't bring himself to look at her and he couldn't stop his mind from racing to picture himself doing – God knows what! – while that ticking measured his performance. Or lack thereof.

She chuckled as she watched the realisation dawning on his face. 'Oh, sweetie, your face is priceless. Honestly!' She sat back on the couch and smiled. 'Well, enough about that for now. How's that little wifey of yours?'

* * *

That night he walked into the Japanese restaurant she had stipulated, with his wife on his arm. He was sweating a bit and his heart seemed to be in permanent overdrive ever since he learned she was back. He hoped he didn't have a heart attack.

'I'm glad you wanted to go out for dinner tonight,' his wife was saying. 'But you know Japanese isn't my favourite. Couldn't we have gone back to that little Italian place?'

'Hmm?' he said, his eyes scanning the restaurant for that vibrant hair. He caught a glimpse of her seated at a table near a large picture window as the waiter came over to seat them.

'For two?' he asked.

'Yes, please. Something over by the window, perhaps?' he said, turning to his wife for approval.

'Sure, by the window,' she agreed.

As they followed the waiter, he tried not to stare right at her as they approached where she was seated. As they neared he did dare a look, though. She met his eyes, smiled and said, 'Paul.'

His face burst into flames again. His name was not Paul. But she had named him last time: subPaul. He looked at his wife and she looked back, confused.

He stood like the proverbial deer in headlights, unsure of what to do. But Mistress spoke. 'And this must be your lovely wife.'

'How do you do.'

'Well, I'm fine, thank you for asking. It's wonderful to finally meet you. Paul's told me *so much* about you!'

His wife looked over at him as beads of sweat trickled down his back. He attempted a casual laugh but all that came out was an embarrassing squeak.

'You simply must join me!' she said, as she'd told him she would.

'Oh no, we wouldn't dream of interfering,' his wife started.

'Not at all! I only just got back in town and I'm all alone. You wouldn't have me eat all by myself now that you're here, would you?' she asked, looking imploringly at him.

'No, no, of course not,' he managed to squeak out.

'Wonderful,' she said as they settled across from her and the waiter came to take drink orders.

'Do you eat Japanese very often?' she asked, after the wine had been chosen.

'No, not really,' his wife replied. 'But I do like vegetable tempura, maybe some California rolls.'

'Oh, well, in that case you must allow me,' she said, smiling warmly. 'I spent three years in Japan after college. I know just what you should try.'

'I don't know.' His wife hesitated, looking over at him. She laughed nervously. 'I'm really not very adventurous.'

'No, I've heard that,' Mistress said, quite under her breath, giggling a bit.

'Pardon m–?' his wife started. But then the waiter was back.

She spoke to him in fluent Japanese and he nodded, bowed and wrote on his notepad. Then she turned to them.

'I just ordered an appetiser I have a feeling Paul will like,' she explained. 'Go ahead and order your dinner.'

Once the orders had been placed, she excused herself – 'Have to use the little girls' room!' – and slipped past him.

When she was out of earshot, his wife turned to him. 'Why does she keep calling you Paul? Why aren't you correcting her?'

'Oh that.' He laughed, a slight flush coming back. 'It's just – it's a bit of an in-joke. Like a nickname.' He felt his phone buzz in his pocket. He took it out. Mistress had told him previously he was not allowed to ignore it.

'In-joke? If you say so. Seems a bit rude to me.'

The text was, of course, from her. It was quite long. He tried to read quickly while keeping the screen turned away from his wife.

I ordered salmon sashimi for our app. Raw slices of salmon. When u r about to eat it, pick it up, look at the edge of it, the corner. Imagine that is my little clitty. Kiss it. Put it between

111

ur lips, suck it a bit. Take some time to use ur
mouth on it the way u would my clit. While
ur doing it and imagining my pussy, think about
the fact that this is as close as ur evr going to
get to eating this pussy ur so horny for even
though u've never even seen it. And remember:
I'll be watching.

'Honey? Honey, are you OK?' His wife took her napkin
and put it up to his temple. 'You're sweating. What is it?
Is it bad news? Oh my God, are your parents all right?'

'No, no,' he croaked. He cleared his throat. 'It's fine.
I'm fine. It's nothing, just a work thing.'

'I'm back!' she announced, sliding back into her seat.
'What did I miss? Paul, sweetie, you look like you're
about to pass out.' She leaned across the table and placed
her cool hand on his forehead. His wife looked seriously
unamused. The way Mistress was leaning towards him
he could see right down her top. He got an eyeful of her
lacy red bra, which looked ready to burst open trying to
contain her substantial curves. He saw his wife notice
too. She put a self-conscious hand to her throat.

'I'm fine,' he repeated.

'Oh, that's good. Because, look! The food's here.'

Luckily his wife – who he knew would be completely
unwilling to try anything as foreign and, to her, disgusting
as uncooked pieces of fish – was attempting to make

up for this slight by focusing all her attention on the conversation Mistress was engaging her in. As she feigned interest in Mistress's Japan years, she didn't notice how her husband appeared to be performing cunnilingus on a slice of salmon.

The tiny corner of slippery sashimi really did feel like it could be a clit between his lips. Together with the mild flavour and the faint but pleasant smell of the ocean, it made his cock – which had been stiffening ever since the first sight of her in the restaurant, and then upon reading her raunchy text – grow even harder as he imagined performing this service on the object of his lust. He watched her engaged in her conversation with his wife, knowing she would also be keeping an eye on him through surreptitious little glances. He met her eye on the next glance and swirled his tongue around the fish.

She smiled brightly. 'Paul, you seem to be enjoying the appetiser.' And he nearly swallowed the piece whole as he felt her place her stockinged foot on his crotch under the table. 'You seem to be enjoying it *a lot*!' she said, winking and wiggling her toes on what was now his rock-hard shaft.

'He does like to try new things,' his wife said, giving him a sidelong glance.

'He does,' Mistress said, looking right at his wife with what he could only describe as a mock-serious face. He could see the burst of laughter threatening underneath.

But having his wife wonder why Mistress would laugh at this was the least of his worries. Because things were reaching a crisis point under the table. She kept sliding her foot over his straining dick, back and forth. How could she be so mean? he thought helplessly. She knew his stamina problems, she knew what her feet did to him, she knew that it didn't matter that his cock was trapped beneath his pants and not actually receiving skin-on-skin stimulation. A million thoughts raced through his brain: the salmon in his mouth, her pretty feet in his hands, her mouth near his cock, her gloved hands stroking him. Then his mind jumped to the time she actually made him come in his pants through the hottest email he'd ever read and the vibrations from his car. And that was it.

He let out the tiniest grunt. And gushed.

* * *

As he pulled into his driveway that night, unbelievably glad to be home from his torturous evening, he received another text.

> Over the next weeks u will be learning the rules. Here's 1: u clean up ur mess. YOU. u know what to do.

With a sinking heart he went into his house, into his bathroom, took off his pants, then his underwear. And proceeded to lick.

* * *

Her email the next morning asked him to report to her at her hotel room. He was to make sure he had his stopwatch on. There was really no need to take it off from now on. She said they would be establishing a baseline.

He wasn't exactly sure what that meant. But he had an inkling.

So when he got there he was surprised to find she was not alone.

'Good morning, sweetie! Glad you could join us.' They were sitting on the couch together, looking extremely cosy.

His heart immediately burned with a jealous rage that surprised even him.

'This is Brad,' she said. 'Brad, this is the one I've been telling you about, subPaul.'

He hadn't dreamt it could be possible to experience shame greater than what she'd already produced in him in the past. How incredibly wrong he was. Because when this handsome, tanned, muscular jock in tight pants that left no doubt he was definitely packing a serious weapon, when this 'Brad' turned his attention to him and said, 'Hey,' but with so much knowledge in his stare, he felt he would spontaneously combust. Heat sprang up from behind his eyes. That hot, molten blanket of shame threatened to suffocate him.

She was watching him closely and went to him then. She enveloped him in an embrace and pressed his head down against her soft bosom. 'Shh, shh, now. This is going to be a challenging task, I will admit. But you're ready for it, my sweetie. And it'll be good for you. You'll learn.'

She explained the rules. Brad was going to fuck her. Her 'darling little preemie – short for premature ejaculator, sweetie, it's an endearing nickname!' was going to start his stopwatch, observe and masturbate. She handed him a bottle of lube and said, 'Don't look so miserable, darling. You'll finally get to see me naked!' He had to try to last as long as possible. 'Now don't worry, it's not a contest. Obviously we know you can't last anywhere near as long as Bradley here can.' But he had to last as long as he could to establish a baseline. 'So try your hardest, all right, sweetie? Because we will work with this baseline for the rest of your submission. Trust me, there will be times when you will really wish you lasted longer.' She giggled. 'And also because it will be *really* embarrassing when we compare your pathetic time against Brad's.' She laughed harder. 'But it's not a contest!'

She got undressed then. Both men stared at her,

entranced, as she untied her emerald-green wrap dress and let it fall to the floor. Brad was practically salivating as her voluptuous curves were revealed. She left on her black lace demi-cup bra, matching garters and stockings and patent leather black heels. But she wriggled out of her little lacy panties. Then she went over to the couch and knelt on it, her ample ass swaying alluringly at both men. His first glimpse at her gorgeous pussy revealed shiny light-pink folds already glistening with moisture, her closely trimmed bush framing her entrance. And yes, the carpet matched the drapes.

She turned over her shoulder and said to him, 'Get your lube out, sweetie! Brad and I had a little fun before you got here so we're both ready to go.'

Sure enough, Brad had his enormous cock out and it was in full glory. He wanted to run and hide, so ashamed was he at the prospect of pulling out his less than average-sized dick in front of this monster of a man. Luckily, all of Brad's attention was focused on what he was about to get.

Obediently, he lubed up and started the stopwatch as Brad started to push his enormous rod inside that gorgeous pink flower. 'Oh my God, it's so big,' Mistress cooed. 'Oh, I hope it fits, it's so huge,' she said as Brad put one hand on top of her ass and used his other to massage the tip of his cock into her clit, spreading her wetness around, eliciting even more little groans and sighs of delight from her. 'Mm, at least you wouldn't have this problem of trying to fit it in me, sweetie,' she chimed, as he stroked in misery.

Miserable and jealous as he was, though, his cock was rock hard over the vision of his gorgeous goddess unveiled before him. His eyes drank in the creamy skin of her enormous breasts swaying beneath her as the flimsy demi bra tried to keep them contained. Her hair was up today, giving him a full view of her neck and shoulder blades. He wondered how it would feel to run his hand all the way down her back and over the glorious globes of her ass. The stopwatch ticked away his doom.

Having finally worked his whole cock inside of her now, Brad started to saw back and forth, in and out of Mistress's hole, at what he felt, as he watched, was a pace way faster than anything he could ever manage.

'Now watch Brad here,' Mistress said, as if reading his thoughts. 'He's going at a reasonable pace. Not too fast and not too slow. Mm, yes, that feels so good, Bradley love. Sweetie, what are you doing over there? You're going way too slow! You have to at least match Brad's speed. You're fucking your hand, for goodness' sake. You should at least be able to match his pace.'

The increased speed and her teasing were getting to be too much. He glanced at the stopwatch. Only three minutes! Oh, God, he needed to slow down, stop even, but she forbade it. If Brad could keep going with a real pussy, then he could keep going with his hand. And it looked like stud muffin was only picking up speed.

'Mm, yes! Oh, God, that's good. Come on, sweetie, keep up over there.'

He struggled. He closed his eyes. 'Eyes open, darling, you know the rules.' Oh, God. He opened them. He looked at her. She was getting pummelled from behind by an Adonis. But her eyes were on him.

His hand stroking so fast now felt like it wasn't attached to his body. His brain wanted it to stop so badly. But he couldn't. She didn't allow it. His balls rucked up tight to his body. His seed bubbled. It was no use. No use.

He cried out. They both stared then. Mistress and her lover, four pairs of eyes on his cock as it spurted out the evidence of his failure. And he caught all he could in his hand. So he could clean up his mess.

* * *

If licking his come off his own underwear was bad, then licking his come off his hand while Mistress and Brad watched and laughed was embarrassment Hell. He'd lasted only three minutes and forty-seven seconds. But his torture didn't even end there.

Because Brad went on and on. Brad had stamina the likes of which he knew he could never dream of achieving.

And, horror of horrors, after a while longer of having to sit and watch Mistress get fucked while listening to her tease him mercilessly about his failure, he started to get hard again! And she saw. And she made him stroke again. And, of course, he *still* failed to outlast Brad. Even though it was the second time around. And even though he was only using his hand while Brad got the real thing.

In the end Brad fucked Mistress for thirty-seven torturous minutes, while 'her little preemie' managed to achieve five minutes and sixteen seconds. The third time around. Licking his come up as they laughed that third time made him want the earth to swallow him whole.

But.

As soon as it was over Mistress sent Brad away immediately. Then she gathered him up, took off his clothes and brought him to the bed. He felt weak, drained, so small and helpless. The feeling made him want to lie at her feet and never get up. She lay with him on the bed, caressed his hair, stroked his back. 'Shh, shh, sweetie. It's all over now. No more struggling today.'

And then she did a strange thing.

She took his face in her hands and kissed him softly. And then she gently pushed his head down and guided her nipple into his mouth.

She stroked his hair while he suckled her breast until he was completely soothed and whole once more.

Runaway
Heather Towne

Madame Medieval's place was out in the country, a huge stone gothic house set on a rolling expanse of green grass in the middle of the drought-stricken Texas plains. The woman had a reputation for eccentricity, to go along with her well-known ruthlessness.

I turned off the highway and onto the asphalt ribbon that led up to the house. Then I parked my car, stepped out and walked up to the medieval door of the three-storey castle-like structure. Moonlight illuminated the scene, what looked like candles sputtering from a few windows on the first floor of the house.

Madame Medieval herself answered the crashing bang of the heavy brass door knocker. The woman was even more imposing in person than picture: imperiously tall and slim, with flowing white hair, a smooth planed face bisected by a long aristocratic nose, emblazoned with large violet eyes and a pincushion-red mouth. She was dressed entirely in gleaming black leather, a bodysuit that would have had Catwoman hissing in envy.

'You're late,' she said with a sniff.

'Sorry, I –'

'Come in. Sit down in the parlour.'

She was obviously used to giving orders. And having them obeyed.

I followed her taut leather-clad buttocks down a candlelit marble hallway into the candlelit parlour and took a seat on a red velvet wide-backed chair. She draped herself out on a plush red velvet couch, her bodysuit squeaking slightly.

'You're a pretty little thing – for a bounty hunter,' she commented, crossing her long shiny legs.

I inadvertently reached up and fondled the loose ends of my straw-blonde hair, fluttering my long lashes over my green eyes. My research had told me that compliments were few and far between when dealing with Madame Medieval.

'I get the job done, don't you worry,' I said, breaking free from her commanding eyes, the intoxicating scent of her perfume. 'You've got one for me, I understand?'

She regarded me a moment longer. Then licked her crimson-coated lips and acknowledged, 'Yes. One of my slaves has escaped. I want you to track him down.'

I arched an eyebrow, nothing more.

Madame Medieval rose and swept past me, out of the

parlour and down the hallway. The four-inch spike heels on her black leather boots echoed harshly on the hard floor, leading me on.

She pulled open a heavy oak door, and we descended a wrought-iron spiral staircase, down into her dungeon. More candles sputtered from brass fixtures in the stone walls, casting a flickering light on the various instruments of sexual torture that were scattered about, the devices of depraved sexual deviance and obedience bolted into the walls and the stone floor.

There were three men down there in that subterranean horror chamber as well: one secured by metal cuffs to a giant black leather X; one secured to the wall by a steel chain attached to his studded collar; and one lashed facedown with thick leather straps to a black metal table. They were all starkly naked.

'These are my slaves,' Madame Medieval intoned with a sweep of her arm. She pointed at an old-fashioned pillory, the kind they used to lock the town drunk into for exhibition in the public square about three hundred years ago; empty. 'Minus one, who has escaped.'

I looked the men over. The man clamped to the X was a prominent big-city pastor, Christopher Montgomery, whose Brimstone Cathedral congregation numbered in the tens of thousands, his evangelical television audience in the millions. His naked body glowed pure white, smooth and soft, hard pink cock jutting out from his shaven loins. He had a wispy halo of brown hair and a pleasing middle-aged face. His bright-brown eyes lowered self-consciously when I looked at him.

The man with the collar and chain was a prominent circuit-court judge, Lawrence Johnson, with a reputation for tough justice rugged even by Texas standards. He was down on his hands and knees, his short, compact, deep-black body gleaming. His red mouth hung open, panting, his long neon-pink tongue lolling out. He wore a brown leather muzzle on his hard, handsome face, and his mounded black bottom wagged back and forth as his big brown eyes rolled up at us.

I didn't recognise the third man at first. Until he lifted his head out of the padded hole in the table and cranked it our way. Then there was no mistaking his chiselled brow and dimpled chin, the perfect blond hair and blazing blue eyes: Troy Aikens, local news anchor. His tanned muscular body stretched out six feet four on the table, his huge buttocks humping prominently. He was belted around the shoulders, back, thighs and ankles, his tan cock jutting out down-under through another, smaller padded hole in the middle of the table. Tears of longing misted his telegenic eyes.

'The runaway slave is Carl Diaz.'

I nodded absently, recognising the name: the owner of Diaz Motors, a ten-branch chain of auto dealerships in the metro area.

Then I swallowed the large lump in my throat, the temperature rising in my body and pussy despite the cellar chill, as I thoroughly surveyed the shocking scene, and as Madame Medieval gave each of her remaining slaves a stern look and said, 'You're going to tell Miss Chase everything you know about Carl – why he didn't come home, where he went.'

She turned to me, lifted an ethereally white hand and ran a long, pointed, blood-red fingernail down my cheek. 'They claim they know nothing. But you'll find out; you'll find my slave and bring him back, won't you?'

It was more of a threat than a question, the woman's violet eyes burning into mine, her metallic scarlet lips set in an unforgiving line. I bobbed my head up and down, a shiver running the length of my body, into my pussy, my achingly hard nipples almost piercing the white T-shirt I was wearing under my open denim jacket.

The mistress of the manor ascended the stairs and slammed the door on us.

The three men stared at me, their cocks twitching.

I picked a whip up off the floor and walked over to the Reverend Montgomery. I lashed the nine black leather tails across his heaving chest, and he jerked against the X. 'Where did Carl go?' I asked, lashing him again, flaming red streaks across his creamy-white pecs, flaring his rigid pink nipples even more.

He moaned and flung his head from side to side.

I brought the whip lower, flicked my wrist, wrapped the man's spearing cock with the warm leather tendrils. He jumped, but the metal clamps cuffing his wrists and ankles held him fast. I whipped his cock repeatedly, wrapping it, unravelling, the whipcords singing through the air, his cock blazing up red, swelling longer and thicker with hurt and lust.

Then I suddenly tempered the harsh pain and pleasure with soft, hot, gripping rapture, dropping the cat o' nine tails and grasping the panting man's cock with my bare hand. He cried out, his body arching off the X. His whipped cock beat wildly in the enveloping warmth of my squeezing palm and lacing fingers, his balls bouncing. But he wouldn't, or couldn't, tell me where Carl Diaz had run off to.

I let go of the Reverend's throbbing prick and moved over to Lawrence Johnson. He leapt up on his hands and knees, straining at his chain. Then he watched with glowering eyes and slavering mouth as I slipped off my jacket and let it fall, pulled my T-shirt up over my head and flung it aside. I shook out my blonde locks, my full, tanned, thick-nippled breasts bounding out into the open.

I bent down, spilling my tits into the judge's muzzled face, and picked a black leather strap up off the stone floor. The man lunged at me, shooting his tongue out of an opening in his muzzle and desperately licking at my dangling nipples. I smacked him on the nose with the strap, and he cowered and whimpered.

'Why did Carl leave?' I asked. If they didn't know exactly where the man had gone, perhaps he'd talked to his fellow slaves about wanting to get away, which might provide me with a clue as to his whereabouts.

Lawrence sprang back up, wagging his bottom, anxious to please.

But he didn't say anything, just jerked his head from side to side, his erection jumping between his legs. I smacked him on the nose again. His long tongue shot out of his muzzle again, licked the hurt off his nose this time. I gritted my teeth, unbuttoned my jeans and pushed them down.

He really got the scent now, all the men did – the tangy, musky aroma of my bared blonde pussy – and he knew what the reward would be for any information he provided. Because I kicked my jeans aside and stepped closer, thrust my brimming mound into his face, letting him take a long, wet slurp at my slit, as a treat.

He yelped with joy. I shuddered with pleasure. The man had all the tools of a real dog.

I backed away, out of range. He leapt at me. The chain and collar yanked him back, choking him in mid-air. His eyes bugged out, red-veined, his jaws drooling, his tongue squirming obscenely at me like an engorged, enraged worm. His cock bobbed rapidly up and down. But he didn't tell me a thing.

Troy Aikens had been watching it all from his neck-wrenched position strapped to the metal table. His cock protruded from the underside, the longest, thickest pulsating slab of meat of the three. I picked up a flat wooden paddle as I moved over to him, and brought it crashing down on his ass without warning as I stepped alongside.

The table rattled with my blow and his reaction, his cry rending the stuffy air.

'Who was Carl seeing, besides Madame Medieval? What other mistress was he slave to?'

The hunky news anchor anchored to the bolted table craned his corded neck to look at me, his handsome face burning red, his blue eyes shining, spilling tears of joy. His plush lips parted and his lush mouth opened and closed. But he was just gasping for air, not words. I crushed his padded buttocks with the cricket-bat-shaped paddle a second time, making metal and man whine.

I smashed his ass over and over and over, my breasts shuddering and shimmering, pussy surging and dripping. His butt-skin blazed crimson, blistering under my bat, while my own skin sheened with sweat. He jerked every time I struck him, his head thrusting up, cock out, fleshy back-mounds gyrating with emotion. If he knew anything, he wasn't telling me, perhaps out of fear I might stop the beating.

That's the problem with slaves – their sheer perversity.

I slammed the paddle to the floor. Then I detached the table platform from its legs at the front and back and pushed it upwards, tilting the table and Troy vertical. His cock stuck out from the hole at pussy level in front of me. I turned around and backed up against his prick, grabbed the enormous straining appendage and stuck it in my sodden cunt.

The news anchor and I both groaned. Inflicting all that punishment, tormenting those twisted men, had given me a raging lust that only primed and protruding slave-cock could satisfy.

I bounced back and forth on Troy's prong, splatting my butt cheeks against the table, sucking on his cock with my cunt. He could see me through the face hole, but he could feel me only with his cock, the rest of his sweating body separated from my soft, taut, curvy form by the impenetrable barrier of metal. He cried out, coming inside me after only a minute or so, cock jetting semen.

I jumped forward, off his erupting prick, forcing him to spray the rest of his hot, pent-up passion all over the wall and floor, without the luscious aid of my pussy. I just knew that Madame Medieval would make the man clean up his mess, probably with his tongue.

Lawrence tried to spring onto my back when I went down, doggy-style, in front of him. But I'd measured the distance well with my eyes, and the chain snapped him back, hanging him up over me on my hands and knees, his paws scrambling in the air to reach me. I reached back and slotted his cock into my sticky pussy, and he frantically pumped his hips, fucking me like an animal.

Drool splashed down onto my back, stringing out of his mouth and muzzle. I was rocked back and forth on my hands and knees by the force of his frenzied fucking, his dong pistoning my pussy.

He let out a strangled howl, and I felt hot semen spray my tunnel for a second time. I instantly jumped forward. Lawrence's cock popped out of my pussy and leapt into the air, spouting spunk out the tip in ropes. The judge almost asphyxiated himself before he collapsed to the floor.

Reverend Montgomery's prick was begging for it. Semen oozed out the slit and rolled down the quivering upthrust shaft. I slapped it with my hand, shocking more pleasure into the man's angelic face and cherubic body. Then I crowded right up against him, face to face, pressing my tits into his chest, ploughing his staff into my pussy. Hot, fervent prayers of thanks tumbled out of his mouth into my open mouth, as I gripped his shoulders and undulated my pelvis, fucking myself on his cock.

His hands balled into fists on the X, his legs straining. But he couldn't break his bindings and wrap his arms around my bountiful bouncing body, plunge his hands onto my thick clenching buttocks.

I dug my claws into his shoulders, thumping against

him, fast-fucking the frantic man. Until I screamed in his reddened face, overcome by orgasm myself. Wave after wave of white-hot ecstasy surged up from my cocked cunt and swept through my blazing body.

I staggered back just before he came, leaving him to frustratedly, fantastically spurt all on his own. He blessed that stone dungeon floor with holy seed over and over and over.

* * *

I had to conclude, after my interrogation, that Madame Medieval's slaves didn't know anything about Carl Diaz's whereabouts or plans. The man had simply not come 'home' to Madame's dungeon of servitude one night, but had broken out on his own.

It happened. Not very often, but every now and then a slave ran away from his mistress. Usually at the behest of another beautiful, sadistic woman promising even more brutal treatment. Love or money seldom had anything to do with it.

So I checked around town with all the professional dominatrices and private domestic discipliners. Most mistresses will respect another's right of ownership, will return a runaway slave. Some for a fee, some for the privilege of a particularly savage final session with the escapee, some out of plain professional courtesy.

But for all of my efforts I got nothing but sore feet, a splitting headache and the cloying scent of spilled spunk stuck in my nose.

I interviewed the man's employees, colleagues, bankers, searched BDSM databases and websites, hacked into personal medical and tax records. I posted ads for slaves with Carl's approximate measurements and exact peccadilloes, scanned state auto dealership listings for new hires.

And drew a total blank.

This slave had disappeared. He was free.

Or so Madame Medieval concluded with disgust, when she wrote me a cheque for two weeks' worth of services and then crumpled it up and threw it in my face.

Only I'd taken a personal/sexual interest in the perverse case, and escaped slave Carl Diaz never left the steel-trap confines of my mind.

* * *

I was in Tulsa a year or so later, searching for a bail jumper with an Okie twang, when I spotted a man and woman walking hand-in-hand down the main drag. And something stirred in the back of my mind, and the front of my pussy.

The woman was a southern peaches-and-cream special, petite, soft, with long blonde hair tied back with a blue ribbon, girlish figure clad in a white summer dress. But it was the man who made me sit up in my van and take notice. He was tall and thin, with short, glossy, black hair and light-brown skin, soulful brown eyes and a sensual mouth. He was wearing a grey Sunday suit and a thin black tie. They looked like a young couple just come out of church flushed with the word of God and a wholesome, healthy love for one another.

I zoomed in with my spyglasses. He'd grown a moustache to cover the scar on his upper lip, and the mole seemed to be gone from his left cheek. He'd lost weight, the gold rings and chains and watch, cut his hair, replaced the flashy threads with ultra-conservative attire; but his height was a match, like the rest of his fine facial features.

There was only one way to tell for sure.

They spent an hour window-shopping, wandering into a couple of maternity stores, before getting into a grey Ford subcompact and putt-putting out to a modest bungalow in the 'burbs. There was a white picket fence and everything.

The guy doted on the young lady, opening the car door for her and then the front door of the house, before devotedly following her inside.

I played it patient, keeping my post out in the van kerbside. There was no need to get innocent civilians mixed up in it. That was the first rule of the bounty hunter. I only wanted the runaway.

My patience and sore bum were finally rewarded at

two-fourteen in the morning, when a man slipped out the front door of the bungalow and trotted down the steps over to the garage, where he slowly and carefully heaved up the metal overhead door.

'Going somewhere, Carl?' I asked, as he was about to start his vehicle.

He jumped, stuck his handsome head out the open car window. I flicked on the overhead light, and his eyes went wide as the Texas plains when he saw the costume I was wearing.

A gleaming satanic-red PVC bodysuit was moulded to my womanly form without a stretch to spare. It skinned all the way up to just under my chin, painted to every curve and swell, plunging right down and into the shiny, knee-high, red-leather laced boots strapped to my feet and calves. The platform heels shot me up another four inches or so, adding to my towering, powerful impression, matching the red riding crop accessory I carried in my right hand and smacked against my left palm.

'I – I don't ... who are you? What do you want?'

I smiled evilly. 'Madame Medieval sent me. She wants you back.'

At the mere mention of his former mistress's name, his eyes widened even more, and his lips trembled violently. He spluttered, 'I don't know anyone by th-that name! Please – please get out of my garage! I'm just ... going out for a drive!'

134

I slammed the crop against the side of the car, making him jump. 'Madame Medieval said I'm to punish you for running away. So get out of that car, get down on your hands and knees – and lick my boots.'

He fell out of the vehicle. It was all too much for his servile nature to resist. He *had* to obey. He hit the concrete and crawled over to me as fast as his hands and knees would carry him.

'You're Carl Diaz?'

He looked up at me, scared, shivering, compliant and caught. He nodded.

I stuck out my right boot, and he stuck out his thick pink tongue and licked the hard, rounded tip of my stomper. Identification: complete.

His tongue swirled all over my boot, anxiously washing the shaped leather. I smacked his head with the flexible rubber end of the riding crop, and he licked my other boot, just as urgently. My feet shone with his spit-polish.

I smacked him on the head again. He glanced up at me, his eyes glassy. I reached down and tilted his chin painfully higher with the tip of the crop. 'Now, lick my legs. Up to my pussy.' I flicked his chin away.

Carl's tongue squeaked against my one boot, ardently slurping upwards. He lapped up my other boot, painting the ankles and shins of the pair with excited saliva. His tongue shot onto the PVC material, strongly dragging along my second skin, higher and higher. Until his licker landed on the crotch of my bodysuit and feverishly stroked up and down.

I shuddered at the sexual impact. I could feel the heavy lap of his eager tongue on my brimming slit through the thin suit, the budded texture of his huge mouthorgan, the heated wetness on my heated wetness.

My pussy tingled outrageously under his licking tongue. I smacked him on the head just in time, before I lost it. 'Lick my tits!' I rasped.

He shot his hands up and onto my hips, thrusting his head high, surging his tongue all over and around my left breast, then my buzzing right boob. I quivered with the strength of his obsession and obedience, his tongue swelling my breasts, stiffening my nipples. When he suddenly licked up my chest to my chin, seeking my wet, open mouth, I barely managed to smack him back down again.

But I did smack him down, swatting him hard on the nose with the crop. He jerked his head back and dropped to his knees. 'Take off your clothes,' I ordered.

He peeled off his green polo shirt and khaki chinos, then his white undershirt and underpants. Until he knelt naked before me, his false identity stripped clean. His long, smooth, tan cock sniffed up into the air from his loins, straining for my cunt, or worse.

I smacked his hard-on with the crop. His body jerked, his face twisting with raw pain and pleasure. Despite his pretence of normalcy, he had been completely exposed for the abuse-seeking, submissive pervert he really was. I whipped his cock from one side to the other, spanking his rigid manhood.

'Stand up, turn around, put your hands up against the car.'

He jumped up and spun around and pasted his sweaty hands to the trunk of his drab domestic vehicle. His buttocks stuck out as far as his cock, twin tan orbs that shone under the illuminating wattage of the single lightbulb. I slashed them with the crop, right across the trembling pair.

He groaned, arching his body, sticking his bum out even further. I strolled alongside the naked man in my high-heeled boots and whistled the whip down onto his ass. He vibrated with depraved passion, his butt cheeks gyrating. I stung him again and again and again, searing red streaks across his rounded back-flesh.

'Lie down on the floor! I'm going to ride your cock!' I was shaking almost as badly as he was, my body ablaze in the suit, pussy seeping arousal.

Carl stumbled back from the car and crumpled down to the hard floor, stretched out on his back, wincing slightly as his heated buttocks met cool concrete. His cock jutted up over his stomach, standing tall, his eyes locked on mine.

I picked up his undershirt and dropped it onto his

face. 'Tie this around your head, cover up your eyes!' He had no right to see me deriving any pleasure from his well-deserved humiliation.

He quickly blindfolded himself, and I unzipped the slit in the crotch of my crimson bodysuit, squatted down on top of the laid-out man. He whined when I rasped his dick through the steel teeth of the zipper, whimpered when I plunged his cock into my pink velvet tunnel. I sat down on him, burying his cock inside me.

I whacked his chest with the crop, started bouncing up and down on his prong, riding the moaning man. My boots scraped on the pavement, my breath coming in hisses between clenched teeth, tits jumping, pussy sucking on the cock filling and churning my tunnel. He lay as still as he could, as I'd ordered, his arms rigid at his sides, his lip bleeding where he bit it, his eyes just about burning through the blindfold.

Whipping him faster and harder, I rode him faster and higher, bounding up and down on his cock. My bum cheeks splashed against his clenched thighs, the rubber crop-tip lashing at his chest. I was catapulted up and away, heavenward (despite my outfit and actions), wet wicked orgasm sending me blissfully sailing; propelled by the furious hot spurts from Carl's cock going off in my cunt.

I didn't let him leave even a note for his slumbering newly betrothed, nor pack a bag. We didn't have time for such foolishness. Madame Medieval was waiting back at his home dungeon, impatiently. She would provide for him, punishing him severely.

He cried out his full confession as we barrelled through the warm black Oklahoma night into Texas. He'd escaped from his mistress, yes, fled the state, found a new job and started a new life with a woman who actually loved him. But had he escaped his true twisted nature? I just shook my head. Not a chance.

When I'd caught up with him he'd been on his way away from his blushing bride for a 3 a.m. session with Lady Jane Pain, to be strapped to a table and face-sat, pissed upon, among other assorted debaucheries. Because for him and his pathetic like, slave isn't a word, it's a way of life, and always will be.

Confessions of a Coffee Slave
Lisette Ashton

Today

Sian placed the tray of coffees down in front of him. It was an act that verged on being ceremonial. In the fashion of a supplicant she lowered herself to one knee and then settled the drinks on the table. Her expression remained sufficiently tight-lipped to contain her smile. She kept her gaze fixed on Walter's eyes so as not to reveal any of her thoughts.

'Thank you,' Walter muttered.

The reporter beamed gratitude at Sian and then went back to scribbling notes in her pad. She appeared to have missed the importance of the way the coffee had been delivered. She seemed oblivious to the fact that coffee serving was something of a ritual in the house of the man who wrote *Arabica*.

'You have to tell me about your home life,' the reporter gushed. 'Our readers will be desperate to know.' Pointing the end of her pen in Sian's direction, she asked, 'Who's this? Is it your girlfriend? Your wife? Or is she just some lucky assistant you have who makes your coffee?'

'Sian?' Walter purred with a smile. 'She's my coffee slave.'

The reporter chuckled as though it was the funniest joke she'd ever heard.

Sian fixed Walter with an inscrutable expression.

'Perhaps I should interview her?' the reporter suggested. '"Confessions of a Coffee Slave",' she joked. 'Do you think that would make for an interesting article?'

Walter seemed to consider the suggestion. 'I think talking about my latest book will make for a more interesting article,' he admitted. 'But then – what would I know? You're the reporter. I'm just the best-selling author.'

The reporter and Walter laughed together and Sian said nothing. She only studied him in silence, a patient coffee slave waiting to see if her offerings were met with approval or disdain. She squeezed her thighs tight together as she anticipated the various ways he might respond to what she'd brought him.

After a year with Walter, she thought she knew what she could expect.

One Year Earlier

They met at a book signing. There had not been as many people there as Sian expected. It was, she thought,

141

almost as though people had stopped reading books and no longer appreciated the genius of a literary giant like Walter Archer. She pushed that idea from her mind, sure that such a state of philistinism was unthinkable.

Getting close to her idol had been comparatively easy.

She had waited in an embarrassingly short line of book buyers who were all expecting the author to sign copies of his latest publication. She had slipped a sleek silver pen into his fingers and, even though he was there to promote *Robusta*, his latest book, she had asked him to sign her copy of his breakout bestseller, *Arabica*.

Sian had been the last in the short line.

She hadn't minded waiting for him to finish chatting with the few fans who had turned up to the signing. She had eavesdropped casually as readers told him how much they'd really enjoyed *Arabica* and how those snippets of *Robusta* they'd found online had already caught their interest and they were sure this book was going to be as sensational as its predecessor.

Sian hugged her copy of *Arabica* against her breasts while she waited, comfortable with the knowledge that being last in line meant she would have a greater chance to monopolise his time while he scribbled her name inside the cover.

As Sian told Walter about her favourite parts in the novel, she accepted his invitation to share a cup of the bookshop's reputed caffè corretto. It was no longer enough for a bookshop to sell books and introduce authors to an audience of readers, Sian thought. Nowadays they needed to sell cappuccinos and lattes and espressos as well as books.

But, ever the optimist, she realised that the combination of bookstore and coffee shop meant she would have longer to spend in the company of Walter Archer.

She had made her decision then and there.

If the opportunity arose, she would fuck him. No matter how depraved his requests might be, no matter how demanding he turned out to be, she would do whatever Walter asked of her. The thought made the muscles between her legs turn to liquid heat.

'I loved the sexual relationships in the novel,' she confided.

She had thought it would be embarrassing to make that admission. It was tantamount to explaining that she had read his words from a page that was quavering in her left hand while the fingers of her right hand rubbed vigorously against the wetness of her sex.

But, instead of being embarrassed, she found it was liberating to make the statement. It was a book that had defined her sexual needs and she was not going to hide her personal truth from the story's author. 'The sexual relationships were so realistic,' she told him. 'And they seemed to be so fulfilling.'

'I worried about the sex scenes,' he said. 'I wanted them to be convincing and graphic and larger than life. But

143

I didn't want them to come across as being gratuitous.'

'Gratuitous? What does that mean?'

He frowned for a moment as he struggled to provide a definition. 'Not necessary,' he explained eventually. 'Unwarranted.'

She considered him from beneath heavily lidded eyes and said, 'I thought they were wholly warranted.'

He graced her with a knowing smile. 'You sound as though you approve of the dynamics of a master-and-slave relationship?'

'I wanked to it,' she told him. 'I wanked over the book several times.'

The words sat between them like a challenge.

Walter regarded her in a sphinx-like silence.

Sian kept her features composed into a blithe mask, enjoying the suggestion of discomfort in his stiffening posture and trying to work out what he might be thinking and where she could now take the conversation.

She was the first to speak.

'Since I've read about Arabica's adventures, I've been desperate to find someone who will share a relationship like that with me. I've been looking to find a master for my servitude.'

She tilted her jaw in a challenge.

'Where have you been looking?' he asked coolly.

'To be honest, I decided to start my search here, tonight.'

'Perhaps I should give you a trial?' he suggested.

They were sitting side-by-side in one of the bookshop's comfortable settees. There was a coffee table before them and Sian's signed copy of *Arabica* sat there waiting to be transported home to take pride of place on the bookshelf beside her bed.

The reading and signing had lasted less than an hour. The modest crowd had quickly dispersed when they saw that Walter Archer was engrossed in the company of the leggy blonde wearing the too-short miniskirt.

Archer's agent, a busy little woman with a BlackBerry planted permanently against one ear, had taken care of the arrangements around them. She had dismantled the promotional signboards announcing that the author of *Arabica* was attending the bookstore to sign copies of *Robusta*, his *New York Times* bestseller. She had already left the shop after a curt wave in Archer's direction and some vague hand-signal that Sian guessed meant they would catch up with one another on the phone. And Sian realised that meant Walter Archer was hers – and hers alone – for the remainder of the evening.

She was definitely going to fuck the writer.

She was making mental plans for how to best go about achieving that goal. But it wasn't until Walter suggested giving her a trial for the role of his Arabica that she realised it would not be difficult to bed him.

'Go and fetch me a coffee,' he said. 'You know my

tastes. Let's see if you're capable of being a sex slave like Arabica.'

'Is that the only way you're going to test my suitability?'

'I think it will do for a start.'

Sian could have climaxed where she was sitting. His words inspired a rush of liquid excitement. She held a breath and then savoured the pleasure of exhaling as she mentally catalogued her situation. She was in the presence of the man whose novel had defined master-and-slave relationships for her. She was chatting intimately with the man whose novel had made her want to experience the thrill of being submissive.

And now he had given her a command.

There had been no 'please' and no 'would you mind?' He had given her an imperative instruction and it was up to her to respond appropriately.

She eased herself from the settee beside him and walked slowly over to the counter at the back of the store.

It was a calculated walk. She was wearing heels that were too high to permit anything less than long measured strides. She didn't doubt that Walter was watching every step, and she suspected he would be hoping that her skirt might ride up high so that he could catch a glimpse beyond the hem and see whether she wore panties, or if she was as naked beneath as any of the torrid characters from *Arabica*.

Knowing that the weight of his gaze rested on her rear, she could feel the heat in her loins begin to broil. Her arousal smouldered as she waited for the drink to be prepared. By the time it was placed on a tray for her, Sian could feel the hard buds of her nipples pressing painfully against the constraints of her bra.

She returned with only a single coffee for him – nothing for herself.

She glided through the shop as though she was serving royalty. Rather than simply placing the coffee on the table in front of him, Sian lowered herself to one knee and offered him the tray with ceremonial reverence.

'You really did enjoy my novel, didn't you?' he said, grinning.

'Several times,' she whispered.

His grin disappeared. His mood had transformed into one of sexual solemnity.

'I could recite parts of *Arabica* verbatim,' she murmured.

His smile returned. 'I think I'd like to hear that. I think I'd like to hear that very much.' He raised the coffee to his lips and then his good mood evaporated with his first sip of the drink.

'Fucking instant?'

He was wiping the back of his hand against his mouth as though trying to expel a foul taste. His lips were wrinkled into a sneer of absolute disgust. 'Do you recall what happened to Arabica when she served the story's hero with instant coffee?'

Sian squirmed silently at his words. She remembered exactly what happened in that particular section of the novel. Even though the words were invariably trembling when she read them, she had gone over them often enough to know them by heart.

* * *

'*Are you trying to earn a punishment?*'

He wrinkled his nose again, as though echoes of the inferior taste were still souring his senses. He'd been expecting caffè corretto. In its place he'd got store brand instant blend. Arabica caught a breath as she heard the fury in his voice. The molten heat between her thighs turned into a river of lava.

'*I'm going to bend you over my knee,*' *he told her.*

She gasped.

The idea made her want to melt for him.

'*I'm going to bend you over my knee and I'm going to spank your backside.*'

She could picture it happening. The prospect left her needing him with such a powerful desire she thought she was going to collapse. Swallowing heavily she asked, '*What will you do once you've spanked me?*'

There was no hesitation in his eyes.

Studying him she knew that he had planned this punishment with a perfect understanding of her need for his sexual domination.

'Once your backside is blazing red …' he began.

She tried not to tremble. She didn't want him to think she was too eager to suffer his abuse.

'… and once I think you've had as much as you can take, I'm going to let you suck my dick by way of an apology.'

'Very well, Master,' Arabica told him.

* * *

'I remember that part of the novel,' she admitted.

She raised her gaze to meet Walter's and struggled not to smile for him.

'Do you remember what Arabica had to do to make up for that offence?'

Keeping her expression as neutral as her excitement would allow, she said, 'I remember that part very well, Master.' Unable to stop herself, Sian drew her tongue over her lips while she continued to meet his gaze.

Walter beamed at her.

He stood up and slid an arm around her waist.

Sian was delighted to see the shape of his erection thrusting at the front of his trousers. With different dynamics to their burgeoning relationship, she would have reached over and touched the shape of his arousal. But because she was being servile to his mastery, she knew such contact would have been inappropriate.

Walter had not yet given her permission to touch him so intimately.

He led her to the desk where she'd bought the coffee. He found the manager and asked if he could make use of the privacy of one of the shop's offices. The manager was reluctant until Walter pushed two twenties into his hand.

The offer of a third twenty sealed the deal.

It was claustrophobic in the manager's untidy office. It was not a large room. And there was no window. But it was secure and private and, she realised, they were alone together.

She half expected him to kiss her.

She thought he would take her in his arms and treat her to the sort of exploratory kiss that she'd read of at the climax of a thousand romantic novels. Even though she knew he wrote fiction with a more passionate and forceful edge than mere romance, a part of her had expected the physical excitement of his lips pressed against hers and his arms taking her in a secure and warming embrace.

Instead he said, 'Bend over.'

She could not have felt greater excitement if he had slipped a finger into the boiling centre of her sex.

'Bend over now and prepare to be punished for your offences.'

'My offences?' she challenged.

'Serving me that filth and pretending it was coffee.'

She shivered. It sounded like another line from *Arabica*. If she'd thought about it she might have remembered where the line came from. But there were more pressing matters demanding her attention.

She did as he asked.

She straightened her spine first. She wanted to let him admire her slender curves and the form-fitting attire she wore. She also wanted to savour every moment of the punishment that was coming and she knew that this would be the ideal way.

Throwing her shoulders back and her chest forward, she turned so that her rear was facing him – and so that she could move her legs and plant her feet apart, hip-wide.

Then, with deliberate and measured slowness, she began to lean forward.

She bent from the waist.

Her legs and backside were immobile, although she suspected it looked like her rear was rising to meet Walter.

'Very good,' he murmured.

The praise alone would have warmed her. But, as he said the words, she felt his fingers fall to the cheek of her backside. His hand was only caressing the black cotton fabric of her miniskirt. It wasn't the intimate connection of skin-on-skin. But it was still a contact that roused a tantalising rush of thrilling and illicit responses.

151

A thrill of raw excitement shivered through her sex.

She struggled valiantly to make sure her legs didn't tremble or show any sign of weakness from the euphoria that came with his caresses.

'This is a very short skirt,' he muttered.

His hand remained in contact with her rear but the fingers smoothed downwards. His fingertips reached the hem and the electric contact of his touch brushed at the tops of her thighs. She hadn't realised how short the miniskirt was until his finger traced against her flesh. It felt as though he was drawing an invisible line against the curve of her buttock.

Her heartbeat raced.

She shivered at his touch and knew that the thrill of a climax was going to be hers. His finger slipped from side to side. It was the most pernicious form of teasing she could imagine. The muscles inside her pussy ached with their need for him. It took every effort of Sian's willpower to contain the urge to groan.

'But,' he said idly, 'even though this skirt is very short, I can't spank you while you're wearing it.'

'No.' With a supreme effort she managed to keep her voice flat and bereft of intonation. 'I don't suppose you can.'

'So I'm going to have to move it aside,' he explained.

She said nothing.

She remained bent at the waist, waiting for him to

continue controlling the situation. She supposed it would have been sensible to agree on a safe word before taking things to this level. Since reading *Arabica*, she had read enough about the practicalities of master-and-slave relationships and the dynamics of sexual submission and domination. She had researched the subcultures online and through a dozen different novels and weighty tomes of lifestyle literature.

But common sense told her that she had no need to discuss safe words with Walter Archer. He had written the book that gave a shape to her desires. The idea that she would need to stop him at any point was unthinkable.

He began to peel her skirt upwards.

She wanted to groan.

His strong hands were on the hem of her skirt, smoothing the fabric upwards. His fingers stole over the rounded mounds of her buttocks, pushing the fabric away. She could feel the material tightening against her stomach. And, when she heard his gasp of approval, she knew that Walter was staring at her bare and exposed backside.

'You took the novel very seriously, didn't you?'

'I take everything very seriously,' she replied.

She tried to imagine the sight he would have. She knew her backside was one of her best features. The muscles of her rear were rounded and well formed. The curve of her buttocks would be broad and their shape would lead to the invitation of her cleft. The puckered muscle of her anus would be on display to him and, she suspected, he would be able to see the smooth and hairless expanse of her pussy lips.

She figured her labia would be pouting at him from between her parted thighs. She wondered if the lips were still clinging together with the moisture he inspired, or if her sex had opened as though sighing in appreciation at his mastery.

His fingers brushed lightly against one bare cheek.

She felt momentarily lightheaded, sure that the pleasure would prove too much. She wondered if she should tell him that she was in danger of passing out from the excitement of suffering his command over her unworthy body.

And then he landed one hand hard against her rear.

The sound rang hollowly from the dusty walls of the manager's office. It was not the loudest sound she had expected to hear. In truth, it was no more than a light slap. But its echoes reverberated through her body.

She held herself still for him, silently willing that he would land his hand against her for a second time.

He did.

This time there was more force behind the blow.

She could imagine that this slap was leaving a palm-print of red flesh blazing against the paleness of her rear. The blow came with such force she could feel the air momentarily pushed out of her. And when she did draw a shocked breath to replace it, she heard it come in a gasp of pleasurable surprise.

'You should never serve instant coffee to any man,' he said solemnly.

'No, Master,' she agreed.

He chuckled. 'Do you think you've learned your lesson?'

'I think I'm learning,' she whispered.

His hand fell hard against her for a third time. This was the most powerful blow of all. And with it she felt the first blistering wave of her climax. He had been striking with his right hand against the right cheek of her backside. Now he slapped the left cheek of her buttock.

Sian would have been dizzied by the shock of his palm sparking life into her rear with this punishing blow. But the tips of his fingers grazed the lips of her labia.

She didn't know if the contact was calculated or an accidental caress.

Either way, the results were the same. She was stung by the thrill of his fingers pressing against her sex and the orgasm rushed through her body.

A ripple of raw excitement flooded from the lips of her sex and soared to her extremities. She felt the harsh impact of his hand slamming against her rear. But that pain was cushioned by the caress of his fingertips slipping against the soft and yielding flesh of her sex.

She had known she was aroused. She had known her

body was desperate for his caress. But she had not realised she was so desperate for the cataclysmic flood of
this release. The cry of gratitude came unbidden from her
throat. She held herself stiff as the eddies of joy trembled
through her frame. And she shivered as the explosion of
wetness rushed from her loins.

Walter chuckled softly.

She felt him draw a finger against her sex.

The touch, a slippery silken caress against her tingling
labia, was almost too much. She feared that the contact
might cause another rush of pleasure. And she held herself
rigid, unsure if her body could cope with so much excitement so soon after such a magnificent climax.

He eased his finger away before the contact became
unbearable.

'Now you may suck my dick by way of apology,' he
told her.

She raised herself slowly and then turned to regard him.

It was no longer difficult trying to keep her features
inscrutable. She was playing the role of his slave and he
was playing the role of her master. And it was a role-
playing game she intended to enjoy for a very long time.

Holding his gaze, Sian knelt before him.

She unzipped his trousers and took his erect length
into her fingers. Inhaling the scent of his excitement,
she slipped a tentative tongue against his stiffness and
then circled him with her lips. She sucked hungrily on

his erection and realised she had found her vocation in life. She only hoped there would be a way to convince Walter that her submission to his mastery was something he needed.

A knock landed lightly upon the manager's door.

'Are you going to be long in there, Mr Archer?'

Sian responded. She moved Walter's cock from her mouth and said, 'We'll be out in two minutes. Could you prepare Mr Archer a caffè corretto, please, before we leave?'

And, when he smiled down at her, she knew that he needed her as much as she needed him.

Today

Walter took a sip from his drink and grimaced.

'Instant?' he muttered. 'Fucking instant?'

The reporter looked up, frowning. She started to ask if there was a problem but Walter ignored her. His attention was fixed on Sian.

'Did you know you brought me instant coffee?' he demanded.

She met the challenge of his gaze with an inscrutable smile.

Dominant Skin
Aishling Morgan

'Welcome to my boudoir,' the Mistress said. 'As you are a woman, you may sit.'

'And if I was a man?' the reporter asked.

'Men,' the Mistress stated, as she took her place on a gold and red throne, 'should be at a level appropriate to their status, on the floor. My slaves are not permitted the use of chairs. However, in certain circumstances, they can be the chairs. Would you like one to sit on?'

'Er ... no, thank you,' the reporter began, eyeing the three men who knelt on the far side of the room with their heads bowed and their hands folded in their laps.

'I insist,' the Mistress continued, and snapped her fingers. 'You, Dreg, make yourself useful.'

One of the three men crawled eagerly forward. He was dressed entirely in black, a body suit that covered him from head to toe, with slits for his eyes and a zipper across his mouth, but with one highly disconcerting detail. His cock and balls were visible, encased in a chastity device of transparent plastic that swung heavily beneath his belly as he moved. The reporter hesitated as he got into position, acutely conscious of her bottom as she lowered herself onto his broad back. She could feel his body heat through the thin rubber gimp suit, and knew full well that the same would be true in reverse, but the Mistress was notoriously precious about her way of life, and it was essential to get the interview.

'Thank you,' she said, 'and that brings me to my first question. I understand that you believe in female superiority.'

'Absolutely,' the Mistress answered. 'Is it not plain to see? Look at woman: beautiful, elegant, poised, intelligent. And then look at man: a shambling brute driven only by lust and violence. Believe me, the world would be a far happier place if men acknowledged their true position, which is as slaves to womankind.'

'I see. And you put this philosophy into practice in your own household?'

'I do. I keep three slaves at present, as you can see. They are all far happier than before they came to me, simply because they have come to accept their natural role. We live in an unnatural world, you see, in which the matriarchy is rejected, with inevitably unhappy consequences, but here all that changes. Take Dreg there.

Before he came to me he had been through two unhappy marriages, both of which foundered on the conflict within him, between taking that place expected of him by our rotten, patriarchal society and his desire to give in to his true feelings and accept his status as a slave. He has now achieved true happiness, in the only way possible for a man, at the feet of a dominant woman. Haven't you, Dreg?'

Dreg nodded earnestly, a movement that caused him to shiver beneath the reporter, making her more acutely conscious than ever of the way she was seated.

Professional to the last, she continued. 'So all three live here as your slaves? Perhaps you could introduce them, for my readers?'

'If you wish, although I wouldn't normally trouble. It's important to realise that males are essentially inter-changeable, aside from physical characteristics, and have no real personality. However, I have given them names, if only to tell them apart from one another, purely for the sake of convenience, you understand. You are seated on Dreg, while the others are Worm and Fleaspeck. Worm, Fleaspeck, you are privileged to greet this lady.'

Both slaves immediately put their foreheads to the ground, then returned to their kneeling positions, neither speaking. The reporter wasn't sure which was which, but despite the Mistress's comments they clearly had some individuality. One wore a zipped and studded leather hood but was otherwise naked but for his chastity device, his strong, muscular limbs and torso bare in a way she couldn't help but find more threatening than submissive. The other was clearly older and softer, although an unnervingly realistic horse's head disguised his features. He had a distinct paunch, while his chastity device hung from the fly of a pair of highly incongruous white underpants.

'And the four of you live in harmony?' she asked.

'Oh, absolutely. They have their little jealousies, of course, stupid things that they are, but I don't put up with any nonsense.'

'I'm sure you don't. If it's not too indelicate a question, may I ask which one you actually sleep with? Who's your partner?'

'I am their Mistress. They are my slaves, to do with as I please, but I sleep alone. This is not something I will discuss further. The night is … different.'

'OK. Now, I understand you give corporal punishment?'

'It is necessary at times, yes,' the Mistress answered, reaching out to take hold of a short flexible whip. 'Generally just a little touch of my friend here is sufficient, but I do maintain a punishment regime, whereby their inevitable mistakes are corrected at the end of each week.'

'What sort of mistakes are these?'

'Oh, you know what men are like, clumsy, foolish creatures who think of very little but food and sex. I keep them in chastity, of course, but, if I find any evidence of excitement, that is sternly punished.'

'But surely everything you do is based around sexual gratification?'

'Good Goddess no! That's a popular misconception, no more. This is not a brothel!'

'No, of course not. I am sorry. So … no sex then?'

'No. They worship me, naturally, but they are not permitted to touch me.'

'So you can state categorically that you do not provide them with sexual relief?'

'Just the opposite. I teach them chastity.'

'I see, but – and I hope you will take this as a compliment – your appearance is highly sexualised, in what many people would consider a … a way that reflects masculine erotic fantasies.'

'I am beautiful. I dress to reveal my beauty. You must, surely, understand that what men mistake for a mere set of pleasing curves is in fact the ethereal perfection of the Goddess's body?'

'Right, er … well, what the readers of my magazine would really like to know about is your outfits. You always dress in rubber?'

'Always.'

'And from head to toe?'

'Yes. Rubber is ideal in many ways, but, most importantly, it is the only material with which I can display my figure to perfection while avoiding any possibility of accidental contact.'

'So your slaves aren't even permitted to touch you, despite the fact that you ... well, some might say you flaunt yourself.'

'Please understand. A woman should never hide her figure, which is to submit to masculine control, and quite unthinkable for me, but man is never, ever worthy to touch a woman's body. That is the significance of what I wear, a second skin, if you will, that allows my slaves to appreciate the beauty of my form, which is of course utterly unobtainable to them. I recommend it to you.'

'I'm not sure I'd have the confidence to wear it,' the reporter answered. 'Please may I take a photograph?'

The Mistress responded with a gracious nod, straightened her back and lifted her chin, posing as the slaves looked on in trembling awe. Her scarlet rubber catsuit fitted extraordinarily well, following every contour of her slender yet intensely feminine body, with reflected highlights picking out the roundness of her breasts and the length of her thighs. Even her head was encased, with her hair rising from the top in a high blonde ponytail, just her face bare, while her short red boots were an exact colour match for the rest of the outfit.

The reporter took several photographers before the Mistress rose to show herself off in different poses: standing with her whip, alone and then with one booted foot on the back of the slave with the horse's head, then seated on the back of the more muscular one, with the sting of her whip trailing across his naked buttocks, and lastly showing off her rear view in a fashion it was impossible to think of as anything but sexual, with the brilliant-red rubber clinging to her bottom and the lips of her sex as if it had been painted on.

As the Mistress took her place on the throne once more, the reporter was left feeling more uneasy than ever, her stomach fluttering at what she could only think of as an intensely sexual situation, which was both frightening and arousing. Her readers, she was convinced, would share her feelings, although probably not the Mistress's philosophy.

'And you have several different outfits?' she asked.

'Dozens,' the Mistress assured her. 'Naturally my slaves like to treat me.'

'I see,' the reporter answered, then asked cautiously, 'But, if they're your slaves, how do they find the money to buy you things?'

'They work, of course,' the Mistress replied. 'Dreg there is an accountant, while Fleaspeck does something in the City. Worm is my houseboy, but I do send him out to strip occasionally, at gay clubs mostly.'

'He is bisexual then?' the reporter asked, realising that Worm was evidently the most muscular of the slaves.

'Oh no,' the Mistress responded, 'not at all. He likes

girls, but it amuses me to humiliate him, and of course it helps to remind him of his place. That's how the three of them get their relief, as well as, when I permit it, by sucking each other's dirty little cocks. I think obligatory homosexual acts are very important for men, because it keeps them in their place, because there is an amusing irony in turning their pathetic desperation for sex onto each other, and because it makes up for centuries of women being obliged to perform with each other for the amusement of men. I enjoy it too, which is even more important. My pleasure comes first, always, and quite regardless of theirs.'

The reporter responded with a solemn nod, having ingested rather more information than she'd bargained for. There also seemed to be several contradictions in the Mistress's philosophy, but she carried on. Her piece had been meant to focus on the Mistress's taste for rubber fashion, but she was finding that the three slaves exerted a worrying fascination, if only for the thought of how it would be to have a handsome young man who would do anything she said without thought for his own pleasure or convenience.

'And they'll do anything you say?'

'Anything,' the Mistress assured her, 'although naturally that comes within the boundaries of common sense. I am strict, but I am not cruel.'

'But you beat them?'

'I chastise them as necessary, yes. That is not cruel, rather the opposite. They understand that, and, besides, they live to serve me and, if something pleases me, it pleases them.'

As she spoke she had flicked out her whip to catch Worm across his naked buttocks, leaving a long scarlet welt. He barely flinched, but the reporter felt her insides go tight. Now thoroughly uneasy, she decided to have a quick look at the Mistress's wardrobe, if only to give her an excuse to get up, as she could feel her cunt, hot and wet against Dreg's back, adding a burning embarrassment to her woes.

Half an hour later the job was done and the reporter left the Mistress's house with her notes and photographs. These were more than sufficient for the article she'd been commissioned to write, while on the face of it the interview had been quick and simple. Nevertheless, she felt she had earned her pay, and also a good hard fucking from her boyfriend that evening.

* * *

The Mistress eased the zip of her catsuit slowly down, her senses responding to every inch of exposed skin. With the front fully open the inner curves of her breasts showed, slick with sweat and talcum powder, and her belly, bare and vulnerable. She had begun to shiver as she peeled the rubber off her long limbs, ever more exposed, until at last she stood naked, no longer the Mistress but plain Caroline White. The door was securely locked against male intrusion, but that only went so far to reduce her feelings as she carefully washed the catsuit, still naked. Her shower just made things worse, the feel of her body as she soaped herself down keeping her constantly in mind of how men reacted to sleek bellies and long legs, to rounded bottoms and generous breasts. By the time she got out she was no longer able to control the trembling of her fingers, while the towel she wrapped around her body failed to reproduce the feelings of protection and safety she got from the rubber.

Nobody seemed to be about, to her surprise, but the quiet was far from reassuring. She had dealt with the men well, that could not be denied, first humiliating all three in front of the reporter, then giving each her personal attention. Dreg had come first, because he'd already spent the best part of an hour with the reporter's sweetly turned bottom perched on his back, with inevitable consequences. Knowing exactly what he'd need, the Mistress had dropped his key on the floor at her feet and made him lick the soles of her boots before allowing him to pick it up with his lips. Released from chastity, he had immediately begun to masturbate, already in a frenzy as he jerked his cock over the yellow plastic dog bowl beneath him. She had stood over him, cool and amused, flicking her whip at his buttocks and laughing at his helpless, pathetic response to being sat on by a woman. Only when he was near the edge had she mounted his back, allowing him the pleasure of feeling her own rubber-clad bottom pressed to his back as he pulled himself off into the dog bowl.

Worm's torment had begun with having the mouth of his leather hood unzipped and the covers removed from his eyes, to find the key to his chastity belt lying in a small pool of spunk at the bottom of the yellow dog bowl. He'd been obliged to eat the contents in order to retrieve the key, licking up every last speck and stain before she granted him permission to free himself from chastity. As with Dreg, he'd begun to masturbate immediately, on his knees as he looked up at her in dumb adoration, his eyes feasting on the rubber-clad contours of her body. She'd thoroughly enjoyed herself with him, turning slowly to show off the way the rubber followed every curve of her bottom and ducking down to allow him to admire her breasts. He'd grown ever more urgent, and as he began to sigh out her name she had reached out to lift his chin beneath one delicate rubber-clad finger and remind him that he had just taken another man's spunk in his mouth. His answering sob of blended shame and ecstasy as he came in his hand had been like an electric shock, leaving her determined to make Fleaspeck's suffering yet more dramatic.

First she had bound his hands securely behind his back, stripped off his pants and applied six firm lashes to his buttocks. Then, taking the unfortunate slave's chastity key, she had used it as bait to lure him down the corridor, shuffling on his knees and barely able to see for his horse's head. He had been led into the downstairs bathroom, where she had spent a minute or so tormenting him with the key, making him beg to be whipped and promising the key in return, only to add more strokes. Before long his buttocks had become a mess of weals, while his cock had been straining hard against the inside of his chastity device. She had held out the key, just an inch from his face, then casually dropped it into the lavatory bowl.

His efforts to retrieve it had been comic to say the least. He'd tried to do it with his toes and failed miserably, succeeding only in earning himself further whip cuts for having the temerity to rise to his feet. He'd then tried to use the snout of his horse's head to scoop it from the bottom of the bowl, but again only managed to perform a set of antics so ludicrous that she'd had trouble maintaining her reserve. When he'd finally given up, now kneeling in a pool of lavatory water, she'd listened to his pleas for a while, then walked away, laughing.

The consequences of leaving him unsatisfied were inevitable. He had been exceptionally attentive as they made her dinner and went about their chores, all three now locked safely into their chastity devices. She had ignored him, repeatedly granting little favours to the other two: feeding Worm little pieces of chicken and pasta from her open palm, taking her after-dinner dram of malt whisky seated on Dreg's back. Fleaspeck had struggled to control himself, but his ever-rising pain and frustration had been all too evident, and as she prepared herself for bed she was wondering if she'd gone too far. Chastity kept them on their toes, willing and eager to serve, while it was always amusing to take one or more to the very edge, only to deny him at the last moment. It was an established, effective technique for getting the best out of them, but by the time she had gone upstairs Fleaspeck had seemed on the edge of tears. Their keys had been left on the living-room mantelpiece.

Caroline was smiling to herself as she went to the tall mirror on the back of her bedroom door. For a moment she simply contemplated her naked reflection, half critical, half admiring, but fully aware of the effect that what she saw had on men. A touch of cream to her face and she was ready for bed, only to hesitate and apply rather more to her bottom, just in case. Still naked, she turned off the light and climbed into bed, her room now dark save for the faint glow of the city from beyond her curtains, and the occasional shift of oddly shaped shadows when a car went by outside.

For a long while she lay awake, listening, but the house remained silent and eventually she grew drowsy.

Only when she was on the edge of sleep did she sense an irregular movement among the shadows, jerking her awake with her heart hammering in her chest. She sat up, and only just managed to choke off her scream at the sight of the dark shape standing at the foot of her bed. Again the shadows moved and a second figure stood tall and powerful in silhouette against the faint light of the curtains. She tried to speak, but her words came out as a sob when a third figure moved into place beside the second.

A voice spoke from the darkness, harsh and male, faintly mocking. 'Three tonight, Caroline.'

'Three? But I ...'

'Three.'

She went quiet, her naked body shaking beneath the covers, until they were suddenly whisked away to leave her nude and open. A choking sob escaped her lips as the men moved forward to take hold of her limbs and spread her out on the bed, each of them far too strong for her to resist, even had she possessed the will. Soft, strong cords were attached to her ankles and wrists, pulled tight and lashed to the bed, leaving her spread-eagled, her breasts naked to searching fingers, her cunt open and available.

Again a voice spoke from the darkness. 'I licked your boots. Lick this.'

One shadow moved forward and climbed onto the

bed. Male scent caught her nose as he swung a heavy leg across her body. Her eyes popped wide as something soft and bulbous settled against her lips: his balls. She was sobbing as she poked out her tongue, helpless to resist as she began to lick at the wrinkly skin, still barely able to see, save that he had begun to masturbate as she licked his balls.

He spoke again, softer still but yet more mocking. 'That's right, Caroline, lick my balls. Do you know what this is called, darling? It's called teabagging, when a man lowers his balls into a woman's mouth to have them sucked while he wanks off. Do you like that, Caroline, do you like to suck on my balls while I toss off in your face? Come on, get them right in. Open wide, darling.'

She struggled to comply, gaping wide to allow him to lower the fat, pungent sac of his scrotum into her open mouth. He gave a low chuckle at her acquiescence and began to slap his cock into her face and rub the fat, meaty shaft across her nose and cheeks, using her face to help get himself erect. All she could do was suck, helpless to stop it as he masturbated in her face and knowing full well that she would not be let off a single crude detail of her punishment.

'That is good,' he sighed when he was fully erect, 'very good. My balls are right in her mouth, boys, and she's sucking on them like the dirty little tart she is once she's out of her rubber, with my cock jerking right in her face, and now …'

172

He broke off to lift his body, pulling his balls from Caroline's mouth and immediately substituting his cock, pushing down from above to force her to tilt her head back and let him fuck in her throat. She was struggling to cope from the start, her gullet rebelling at the fat cock head poking in down the narrow tube, making her gag and gulp, spit squeezing from around her lips and bubbling from her nose as the fucking got deeper still.

'Now I'm fucking her face,' he gasped, 'right in, down the little bitch's throat. Will this teach you, Caroline? Will this stop you playing your dirty little tricks? I do hope not, 'cause then I wouldn't be able to use you, you filthy little whore!'

On the last word his voice broke to a grunt and he came, deep in Caroline's throat, his wet ball sac slapping on her chin as he fucked her mouth, her muscles in urgent, painful contraction on the meat of his cock as she gulped down his spunk. Not all of it stayed down, despite her best efforts to swallow, and a good deal erupted from her nose and around his cock shaft, leaving her face sticky and wet as he finally withdrew, to paint the last blob of spunk from the end of his cock onto the tip of her nose before he finally climbed from the bed.

She was left gasping in spunk-scented air, dizzy with her reaction to being teabagged and having her mouth fucked, but helpless to do anything about it. There was no respite either, as the second man immediately climbed onto the bed to straddle her waist with his balls and cock resting hot on the now sweat-slick skin of her belly. She could feel the hard, lean muscles of his thighs, and knew who it was even before he spoke.

'You made me eat spunk, Caroline. Another man's spunk, licked up from a dog bowl. What do you suppose I ought to do to you for that?'

Caroline's answer was a faint whimper as he began to masturbate over her belly, rubbing his balls in the gentle depression of her navel as he pulled at his shaft.

'I should have made you lick that tasty little reporter, shouldn't I?' he went on. 'I should have made you lick her cunt, and swallow down her juices while you frigged off on the floor. But I didn't get the chance, so I'm just going to have to give you a taste of cunt juice another way.'

He moved as he spoke, down between her thighs, which were held wide by the tight ropes. All Caroline could do was cry out softly into the darkness as she felt the head of his cock push against her cunt and in, easing well up the already slippery hole. She couldn't help her reaction as she was fucked, gasping and clutching at the air with her fingers, her limbs tight against her bonds, her mouth wide in helpless ecstasy. He seemed eager too, thrusting deep and hard into her body, until she began to wonder if he really meant to carry out his threat.

When he pushed himself so deep that his balls were pressed between the cheeks of her bottom she thought he'd come, only to have him withdraw, still rock-hard as he moved up the bed once more. She began to sob again, trying to keep her mouth closed but her will-power disappeared in an instant when his helmet pressed at her lips, smooth and hot and sticky with her own juices. Her mouth opened wide, his cock went in and she was sucking up everything she could get, even as the shame of being made to do it raged in her head and she imagined herself on her knees before the pretty reporter, licking cunt.

'Yeah, she's doing it,' the man's voice sounded from above her. 'That's right, swallow it all down, you vicious little bitch, and count yourself lucky my cock had only been up your cunt and not your arse.'

He pushed his cock deep as he spoke, his fingers still around the base so that he could masturbate into her mouth. Caroline began to choke, which brought a touch of panic, only for him to pull out with a happy sigh, then speak again.

'Talking of your arse, Carrie. I bet you've lubed up, haven't you?'

Caroline could only manage a despairing groan as his fingers delved between her bottom cheeks to probe at her anus. He gave a dirty chuckle as he found she was already slick with cream as well as her own juices, and quickly got back between her legs. Two quick motions and the knots that held her ankles were pulled free, allowing him to roll her legs high and spread out her bottom to his erection.

She began to whimper as his cock head pressed against her anus, gradually spreading the slippery little hole out on his meat until he was in and she was buggered. Both the other men clearly knew what was happening, pressing close in an attempt to watch her suffer what had always been the final indignity for her, being made to accept a cock in her anus. Yet there was no denying how good it felt, and she was soon moaning and gasping in helpless pleasure, until a sudden flare of light left the room fully illuminated, the man up her bottom and both the others grinning down at her as she was sodomised.

'No, please, at least leave the light off!' she begged.

'We want to watch,' answered the third man, his eyes glittering with lust and his hand wrapped around a massive, straining erection, 'and don't forget, it's my turn next.'

Caroline gave a weak nod and surrendered herself to being watched as she was buggered. He took his time as well, pumping slowly in and out of her straining ring, pulling free to enter her again in full view of his friends and finally masturbating into her open bottom hole to fill her with spunk before jamming himself deep one last time. That left her limp, with thick male come dribbling from her mouth and anus, feeling soiled and used, still with the prospect of being taken by the man she'd tormented and denied.

He was quick to get to work, untying her wrists as he reprimanded her for what she'd done, then inserting his cock into her mouth, cunt and anus in turn. She took it as best she could, trying to suck when he was in her mouth, lifting her own thighs high and wide as she was fucked and turning on her front to stick her bottom in the air for anal penetration, just as he ordered. She got smacked too, her bottom spanked even as he thrust in up her anus, leaving her rear cheeks pink and warm, yet even then he held back from orgasm.

'You … you should have let me come,' he gasped. 'You should have let me come, Caroline, because you know me, and you know what I do to cruel, spiteful little tarts like you, don't you?'

She found herself nodding, unable to speak for the pumping of his cock in her rectum and the firm slaps of his hand across her bottom cheeks. He laughed, and suddenly took her by the hair and forced her to scramble down from the bed, his cock still up her bottom as she ended up in a crawling position on the floor. The others cheered and clapped as she was ridden out of the door, on all fours with her hair twisted hard in his hand and his cock easing in and out of her straining bumhole.

'What was it you called us?' He laughed as he rode her. 'Shambling brutes driven only by lust and violence? Well, you left out one important word, "perverted", as you're about to find out, Mistress. Oh, sorry, you're

Caroline, aren't you, when you're out of your dominant skin, slutty little Carrie.'

Caroline knew where she was going, steered by her hair, down the passage to the bathroom and into position, her head over the toilet, his cock pumping faster up her bottom hole, the others egging him on, then the final, awful moment as her head was pushed down into the bowl.

'There we go,' he grunted. 'That's what you like, isn't it?'

Caroline nodded. With a last, happy grunt he started to come, and at the same moment he flushed the toilet. Water gushed out around Caroline's head, splashing her face and soaking her hair, as she thought how good it was to surrender her protection, how well they'd used her, and how she might be able to push them further still, taking them to their limits before she shed her protective rubber skin and gave herself over to be taken to her own. Her hand went back between her legs, and as she came up, dripping and soiled, she began to masturbate.

www.ingramcontent.com/pod-product-compliance
Ingram Content Group UK Ltd.
Pitfield, Milton Keynes, MK11 3LW, UK
UKHW022300180325
456436UK00003B/164

9 780007 553198